ALFRED HITCHCOCK ASKS— ARE YOU HIS KIND OF PERSON?

Did you spend your childhood picking the legs off insects—and do you still do it?

Do you cut out newspaper photos of ax murders to put in your album—right next to your own Instamatic snapshots?

Do you faithfully attend funerals—whether you know the deceased or not?

Do you possess such invaluable domestic skills as digging a grave in the cellar and removing bloodstains from fabrics?

If so, Alfred Hitchcock cordially invites you to give final proof of your perfect perversity by meeting his ultimate challenge in—

MORE STORIES MY MOTHER NEVER TOLD ME

14 finds in flawless fiendishness

ALFRED HITCHCOCK PRESENTS:

MORE STORIES MY MOTHER NEVER TOLD ME

A DELL BOOK

Published by
DELL PUBLISHING CO., INC.
1 Dag Hammarskjold Plaza
New York, N.Y. 10017

Dell ® TM 681510, Dell Publishing Co., Inc.

ISBN: 0-440-15816-8

Reprinted by arrangement with
Random House, Inc.

Printed in the United States of America

Previous Dell Edition #5816
New Dell Edition
First printing—March 1977

ACKNOWLEDGMENTS

"The Wind," Ray Bradbury. Reprinted by permission of Harold Matson Company, Inc. Copyright © 1943 by Ray Bradbury. Copyright renewed by the author.

"Congo," Stuart Cloete. Reprinted by permission of *Story* magazine. Copyright © 1943 by Story Magazine, Inc.

"Dip in the Pool," Roald Dahl. Reprinted by permission of Alfred A. Knopf, Inc., from *Someone Like You* by Roald Dahl. Copyright © 1952 by Roald Dahl.

"I Do Not Hear You, Sir," Avram Davidson. Reprinted by permission of Kirby McCauley, Literary Agent. Copyright © 1957 by Mercury Press, Inc.

"The Arbutus Collar," Jeremiah Digges. Reprinted by permission of *Story* magazine. Copyright © 1936 by Story Magazine, Inc.

"The Man Who Was Everywhere," Edward D. Hoch. Reprinted by permission of the author. Originally appeared in *Manhunt* magazine. Copyright © 1957 by Flying Eagle Publications, Inc.

"Courtesy of the Road," Mack Morriss. Reprinted by permission of William Morris Agency, Inc. Originally appeared in *Collier's* magazine. Copyright © 1949 by Crowell-Collier Publishing Company.

"Remains To Be Seen," Jack Ritchie. Reprinted by permission of the author and Larry Sternig, Agent, and the copyright owner. Originally appeared in *Alfred Hitchcock's Mystery Magazine*. Copyright © 1961 by H.S.D. Publications, Inc.

"The Man Who Sold Rope to the Gnoles," Idris Seabright. Reprinted by permission of McIntosh and Otis, Inc. Originally appeared in *The Magazine of Fantasy & Science Fiction*. Copyright © 1951 by Mercury Press, Inc.

"Lost Dog," Henry Slesar. Reprinted by permission of Theron Raines, Agent. Originally appeared in *Michael Shayne's Mystery Magazine*. Copyright © 1957 by Henry Slesar.

CONTENTS

INTRODUCTION

UNLESS YOU BEGAN THIS BOOK AT THE BACK AND HAVE been reading your way forward, you have doubtless perceived that it is entitled *More Stories My Mother Never Told Me.* Permit me to observe that this is an absolutely accurate description of the contents. I am prepared to testify in any court of the land that none of these stories was ever recounted to me in any form by my mother.

The reason for this is quite simple. None of them had been written at the time when my mother was telling stories to me.

Still, I do not think that my mother would have told me any of the tales I have gathered here, even if they had been available to her. And I do not recommend that you pass them indiscriminately along to your own younger offspring. They are stories for the developed taste, one that has left behind it the delights of the blunt instrument, the scream in the night, the poison in the decanter of port.

I believe it has become public knowledge that I am addicted to tales that brush the emotions of the reader with a touch of terror, pluck at his sensitivities with a haunting horror, or set his pulse pounding with suspense. I have gone so far as to issue volumes of stories in which I have grouped narratives that seemed to me to distill these emotions in their finest essence.

But in this book I shall not presume to suggest what reactions these stories should call forth from you, the reader. Nor, despite great temptation, will I call your attention to any specific tales. These stories should be approached without forewarning or preconception. Only in that way may their fullest impact be received by sensitive nervous systems.

The one thing that I can promise is that you are in for a full gamut of emotional reactions—barring, of course, the tender sentiments, with which I will have no truck. I have even included a tale or two primarily for entertainment. But do not look upon this as a sign of weakness. Even in these tales there are underlying *frissons* to give a curious relish to the reading. And there are other stories which I consider well-nigh diabolical. Furthermore—

But someone has said that the best introduction is the shortest introduction.

Onward, then!

ALFRED J. HITCHCOCK

THE WIND

Ray Bradbury

THE PHONE RANG AT SIX-THIRTY THAT EVENING. IT WAS December, and already dark as Thompson picked up the phone.

"Hello."

"Hello, Herb?"

"Oh, it's you, Allin."

"Is your wife home, Herb?"

"Sure. Why?"

"Damn it."

Herb Thompson held the receiver quietly. "What's up? You sound funny."

"I wanted you to come over tonight."

"We're having company."

"I wanted you to spend the night. When's your wife going away?"

"That's next week," said Thompson. "She'll be in Ohio for about nine days. Her mother's sick. I'll come over then."

"I wish you could come over tonight."

"Wish I could. Company and all, my wife'd kill me."

"I wish you could come over."

"What's it? The wind again?"

"Oh, no. No."

"Is it the wind?" asked Thompson.

The voice on the phone hesitated. "Yeah. Yeah, it's the wind."

"It's a clear night, there's not much wind."

"There's enough. It comes in the window and blows the curtains a little bit. Just enough to tell me."

"Look, why don't you come and spend the night here?"

said Herb Thompson, looking around the lighted hall.

"Oh, no. It's too late for that. It might catch me on the way over. It's a damned long distance, I wouldn't dare, but thanks, anyway. It's thirty miles, but thanks."

"Take a sleeping tablet."

"I've been standing in the door for the past hour, Herb. I can see it building up in the west. There are some clouds there and I saw one of them kind of rip apart. There's a wind coming, all right."

"Well, you just take a nice sleeping tablet. And call me any time you want to call. Later this evening if you want."

"Any time?" said the voice on the phone.

"Sure."

"I'll do that, but I wish you would come out. Yet I wouldn't want you hurt. You're my best friend and I wouldn't want that. Maybe it's best I face this thing alone. I'm sorry I bothered you."

"Hell, what's a friend for? Tell you what you do, sit down and get some writing done this evening," said Herb Thompson, shifting from one foot to the other in the hall. "You'll forget about the Himalayas and the Valley of the Winds and this preoccupation of yours with storms and hurricanes. Get another chapter done on your next travel book."

"I might do that. Maybe I will, I don't know. Maybe I will. I might do that. Thanks a lot for letting me bother you."

"Thanks, hell! Get off the wire, now, you. My wife's calling me to dinner."

Herb Thompson hung up.

He went and sat down at the supper table and his wife sat across from him. "Was that Allin?" she asked. He nodded. "Him and his winds that blow up and winds that blow down and winds that blow hot and blow cold," she said, handing him his plate heaped with food.

"He did have a time in the Himalayas, during the war," said Herb Thompson.

"You don't believe what he said about that valley, do you?"

"It makes a good story."

"Climbing around, climbing up things. Why do men climb mountains and scare themselves?"

"It was snowing," said Herb Thompson.

"Was it?"

"And raining and hailing and blowing all at once, in that valley. Allin's told me a dozen times. He tells it well. He was up pretty high. Clouds, and all. The valley made a noise."

"I bet it did," she said, sulkily.

"Like a lot of winds instead of just one. Winds from all over the world." He took a bite. "So says Allin."

"He shouldn't have gone there and looked, in the first place," she said. "You go poking around and first thing you know you get ideas. Winds start getting angry at you for intruding, and they follow you."

"Don't joke at him, he's my best friend," snapped Herb Thompson.

"It's so silly!"

"Nevertheless, he's been through a lot. That storm in Bombay, later, and the hurricane in the Pacific islands two months after that. And that time, at Cornwall."

"I have no sympathy for a man who continually runs into wind storms and hurricanes, and then gets a persecution complex because of it."

The phone rang again.

"Don't answer it," she said.

"Maybe it's important."

"It's only Allin, again."

They sat there and the phone rang nine times and they didn't answer. Finally it quieted. They finished dinner. Out in the kitchen, the window curtains gently moved in a small breeze from a slightly open window.

The phone rang again.

"I can't let it ring," he said, and answered it. "Oh, hello, Allin."

"Herb! It's here! It got here!"

"You're too near the phone, back up a little."

"I stood in the open door and waited for it. I saw it coming down the highway, shaking all the trees, one by one, until it shook the trees just outside the house and it dived down toward the door and I slammed the door in its face!"

Thompson didn't say anything. He couldn't think of anything to say, his wife was watching him in the hall door.

"How interesting," he said at last.

"It's all around the house, Herb. I can't get out now, I can't do anything. But I fooled it, I let it think it had me, and just as it came down to get me, I slammed and locked the door! I was ready for it, I've been getting ready for weeks."

"Have you, now? Tell me about it, Allin, old man." Herb Thompson played it jovially into the phone, while his wife looked on and his neck began to sweat.

"It began six weeks ago. . . ."

"Oh, yes? Well, well."

". . . I thought I had it licked. I thought it had given up following and trying to get me. But it was just waiting. Six weeks ago I heard the wind laughing and whispering around the corners of my house, out here. Just for an hour or so, not very long, not very loud. Then it went away."

Thompson nodded into the phone. "Glad to hear it, glad to hear it." His wife stared at him.

"It came back the next night. It slammed the shutters and kicked sparks out the chimney. It came back five nights in a row, a little stronger each time. When I opened the front door, it came in at me and tried to pull me out, but it wasn't strong enough. Tonight it is."

"Glad to hear you're feeling better," said Thompson.

"I'm not better, what's wrong with you? Is your wife listening to us?"

"Yes."

"Oh, I see. I know I sound like a fool."

"Not at all. Go on."

Thompson's wife went back into the kitchen. He relaxed. He sat down on a little chair near the phone. "Go on, Allin, get it out of you, you'll sleep better."

"It's all around the house now, like a great big vacuum machine nuzzling at all the gables. It's knocking the trees around."

"That's funny, there's no wind here, Allin."

"Of course not, it doesn't care about you, only about me!"

"I guess that's one way to explain it."

"It's a killer, Herb, the biggest damnedest prehistoric killer that ever hunted prey. A big sniffling hound, trying to smell me out, find me. It pushes its big cold nose up to the house, taking air, and when it finds me in the parlor it drives its pressure there, and when I'm in the kitchen it goes there. It's trying to get in the windows, now, but I had them reinforced and I put new hinges on the doors, and bolts. It's a strong house. They built them strong in the old days. I've got all the lights in the house on, now. The house is all lighted up, bright. The wind followed me from room to room, looking through all the windows, when I switched them on. Oh!"

"What's wrong?"

"It just snatched off the front screen door!"

"I wish you'd come over here and spend the night, Allin."

"I can't! God, I can't leave the house. I can't do anything. I know this wind, Lord, it's big and it's smart. I tried to light a cigarette a moment ago, and a little draft sucked the match out. The wind likes to play games. It likes to taunt me, it's taking its time with me, it's got all night. And now! God, right now, one of my old travel books, on the library table, I wish you could see it. A little breeze from God knows what small hole in the house, has flipped the cover of the book open and the little breeze is— turning the pages one by one. I wish you could see it. There's my introduction. Do you remember the introduction to my Tibet book, Herb?"

"Yes."

"This book is dedicated to those who lost the game of elements, written by one who has seen, but who has always escaped."

"Yes. I remember."

"The lights have gone out!"

The phone crackled.

"The power lines just went down. Are you there, Herb!"

"I still hear you."

"The wind got jealous of all the light in my house, it tore the power lines down. The telephone will probably go next. Oh, it's a real party, me and the wind, I tell you! Just a second."

"Allin?" A silence. Herb leaned against the mouthpiece. His wife glanced in from the kitchen. Herb Thompson waited. "Allin?"

"I'm back," said the voice on the phone. "There was a draft from the door and I shoved some wadding under it to keep it from cooling my legs. I'm glad you didn't come out after all, Herb, I wouldn't want you in this mess. It just broke one of the living room windows and a regular gale is in the house, knocking pictures off the wall. Do you hear it?"

Herb Thompson listened. There was a wild sirening on the phone and a whistling and banging. Allin shouted over it. "Do you hear it?"

Herb Thompson swallowed drily. "I hear it."

"It wants me alive, Herb. It doesn't dare knock the house down in one fell blow. That'd kill me. It wants me alive, so it can pull me apart, finger by finger. It wants what's inside me. My mind, my brain. It wants my life-power, my psychic force, my ego. It wants intellect."

"My wife's calling me, Allin, I have to go wipe the dishes."

"It's a big cloud of vapors, winds from all over the world. The same wind that ripped the Celebes, a year ago, the same pampero that killed in Argentina, the typhoon that fed well in Hawaii, and the hurricane that knocked the coast of Africa early this year. It's part of all those storms I escaped. It followed me from the Himalayas because it didn't want me to know what I know of it, the Valley of the Winds where it gathers and plans its destruction. Something, a long time ago, gave it a start in the direction of life. I know its feeding grounds, I know where it is born and where parts of it expire. For that reason, it hates me, for I have written books against it, telling how to defeat it. It wants to incorporate me into its huge body, give it knowledge. It wants me on its own side!"

"I have to hang up, Allin, my wife—"

"What?" A pause, the blowing of the wind in the phone, distantly. "What did you say?"

"Call me back in about an hour, Allin."

He hung up.

He went out to wipe the dishes. His wife looked at him and he looked at the dishes, rubbing them with a towel.

"What's it like out tonight?" he said.

"Nice. Not very chilly. Stars," she said. "Why?"

"Nothing."

The phone rang three times in the next hour. At eight o'clock the company arrived, Stoddard and his wife. They sat around until eight-thirty talking and then got out and set up the card table and began to play Black Jack.

Herb Thompson shuffled the cards over and over, with a clittering, shuttering effect and clapped them out, one at a time before the three other players. Talk went back and forth. He lit a cigar and made it into a fine grey ash at the tip, and adjusted his cards in his hand and on occasion lifted his head and listened. There was no sound outside the house. His wife saw him do this, and he cut it out immediately, and discarded a jack of clubs.

He puffed slowly on his cigar and they all talked quietly with occasionally small eruptions of laughter, and the clock in the hall sweetly chimed nine o'clock.

"Here we all are," said Herb Thompson, taking his cigar out and looking at it reflectively. "And life is sure funny."

"Eh?" said Mr. Stoddard.

"Nothing, except here we are living our lives, and some place else on earth a billion other people live their lives."

"That's a rather naive statement."

"True, nevertheless. Life," he put his cigar back in his lips, "is a lonely thing. Even with married people. Sometimes when you're in a person's arms you feel a million miles away from them."

"I like that," said his wife.

"I didn't mean it that way," he explained, not with haste; because he felt no guilt, he took his time. "I mean we all believe what we believe and live our own little lives while other people live entirely different ones. I mean, we sit here in this room while a thousand people are dying. Some of

cancer, some of pneumonia, some of tuberculosis. I imagine
someone in the United States is dying right now in a motor
crash."

"This isn't very stimulating conversation," said his wife.

"I mean to say, we all live and don't think about how
other people think or live their lives or die. We wait until
death comes to us. What I mean is here we sit, on our self-
assured butt-bones, while thirty miles away, in a big old
house, completely surrounded by night and God-knows-
what, one of the finest guys who ever lived is—"

"Herb!"

He puffed and chewed on his cigar and stared blindly at
his cards. "Sorry." He blinked rapidly and bit his cigar. "Is
it my turn?"

"It's your turn."

The playing went around the table, with a flittering of
cards, murmurs, conversation, laughter. Herb Thompson
sank lower into his chair and began to look ill.

The phone rang. Thompson jumped and ran to it and
jerked it off the hook.

"Herb! I've been calling and calling."

"I couldn't answer, my wife wouldn't let me."

"What's it like at your house, Herb?"

"What do you mean, what's it like?"

"Has the company come?"

"Hell, yes, it has—"

"Are you talking and laughing and playing cards?"

"Yes, sure, but what has that got to do with—"

"Are you smoking your ten-cent cigar?"

"Damn it, yes but—"

"Swell," said the voice on the phone, enviously. "That
sure is swell. I wish I could be there. I wish I didn't know
the things I know. I wish lots of things."

"Are you all right?"

"So far, so good. I'm locked in the kitchen now. The
front wall of the house just blew in. But I planned my retreat. When the kitchen door gives, I'm heading for the cellar. If I'm lucky I may hold out there until morning. It'll
have to tear the whole damned house down to get to me,

and the cellar floor is pretty solid. I have a shovel and I may dig—deeper. . . ."

It sounded like a lot of other voices on the phone.

"What's that?" Herb Thompson demanded, cold, shivering.

"That?" asked the voice on the phone. "Those are the voices of ten thousand killed in a typhoon, seven thousand killed by a hurricane, three thousand buried by a cyclone. Am I boring you? It's a long list. That's what the wind is, you know. It's a lot of spirits, a lot of people dead. The wind killed them and took their intellects, their spirits, to give itself intelligence. It took all their voices and made them into one voice. Interesting, isn't it? All those millions of peoples killed in the past centuries, twisted and tortured and taken from continent to continent on the backs and in the bellies of monsoons and whirlwinds. I get very poetic at a time like this."

The phone echoed and rang with voices and shouts and whinings.

"Come on back, Herb," said his wife, at the card table.

"That's how the wind gets more intelligent each year, it adds to its intellect, body by body, life by life, death by death."

"We're waiting for you, Herb," called his wife.

"Damn it!" he turned, almost snarling. "Wait just a moment, won't you!" Back to the phone. "Allin, if you want me to come out there now, I will, if you need help."

"Wouldn't think of it. This is a grudge fight, wouldn't do to have you in it. Well, I'd better hang up. The kitchen door looks very weak and I'll have to get into the cellar."

"Call me back, later?"

"Maybe, if I'm lucky. I don't think I'll make it this time. I slipped away and escaped in the Celebes that time, but I think it has me now. I hope I haven't bothered you too much, Herb."

"You haven't bothered anyone, damn it. Call me back."

"I'll try . . ."

Herb Thompson went back into the card game. His wife glared at him. "How's Allin, your friend?" she asked. "Is he sober?"

"He's never taken a drink in his life," said Thompson, sullenly. "I should have gone out there."

"But he's called every night for six weeks and you've been out there at least ten nights to sleep with him and nothing was wrong."

"He needs help."

"You were just out there, two nights ago, you can't always be running after him."

They played out the games. At ten-thirty coffee was served. Herb Thompson drank his slowly, looking at the phone. I wonder if he's in the cellar now, he thought.

Herb Thompson walked to the phone, called long-distance.

"I'm sorry," said the operator. "The lines are down in that district. When the lines are repaired, we will put your call through."

"Then the telephone lines are down!" cried Thompson, slamming down the phone. Turning, he ran down the hall, opened the closet, pulled out his hat and coat. "Excuse me," he shouted. "You will excuse me, won't you? I'm sorry," he said, to his amazed guests and his wife with the coffee in her hand. "Herb!" she cried at him. "I've got to get out there!" he said.

There was a soft, faint stirring at the door.

Everybody in the room tensed.

"Who could that be?" asked his wife.

The soft stirring was repeated.

Thompson hurried down the hall where he stopped, alert.

Outside he heard faint laughter.

"I'll be damned," said Thompson, pleasantly shocked and relieved. "I'd know that laugh anywhere. It's Allin. He came on over in his car, after all." Thompson chuckled weakly. "Probably brought some friends with him. Sounds like a lot of other people. . . ."

He opened the front door.

The porch was vacant.

Thompson showed no surprise, his face grew amusedly sly. He laughed. "Allin? None of your tricks now! Come on." He switched on the porch-light. "Where are you, Allin? Come on now."

A little breeze blew into his face.

Thompson waited a moment, suddenly chilled to his marrow. He stepped out on the porch and looked uneasily about.

A sudden wind caught and whipped his coat flaps, disheveled his hair. He thought he heard laughter again. The wind suddenly rounded the house and was a pressure everywhere at once, then, storming for a full minute, passed on.

The wind died down, sad mourning in the high trees, passing away; going back out to the sea, to the Celebes, to the Ivory Coast, to Sumatra and Cape Horn, to Cornwall and the Philippines. Fading, fading, fading.

Thompson stood there, cold. He went in and closed the door and leaned against it, eyes closed.

"What's wrong . . . ?" asked his wife.

CONGO
Stuart Cloete

LET THOSE WHO WILL BELIEVE WHAT I HAVE TO TELL; BUT you, Retief, for whom this is written must believe it, for if it comes to your hands her life will be in danger. I, who write, saw this thing, from its small beginning, watched it grow, became involved in it, first as a mere spectator and later in a more intimate fashion. It is therefore no romance but a private part of my life, bringing neither credit nor discredit upon me, and finally coming near to overwhelming me. Indeed as I write, the issue remains in doubt.

As a young man, I was a pupil of the famous Le Grand, at the University of Brussels. By a lucky accident, he once selected me to help him in a small experiment, and found me to be sympathetic to him. I looked at the phenomena of life from his own angle. We saw the same view, through different pairs of glasses; his field of vision being enormous, embracing subject after subject as if they were ranges of mountains; while I saw only a small piece of it, but that I perceived very clearly and with great intensity. It was this gift which endeared me to him rather than any particular brilliance on my part, and led him to choose me as his assistant, in which capacity I went with him to the Congo. We had conducted sufficient experiments in the Royal Botanical Gardens to obtain financial assistance from the Société de Recherche Scientifique, and a grant from the Aide Commerciale des Produits Tropicales; so with what to scientists seemed unlimited economic resources behind us, and armed with every kind of authority, we proceeded to that abominable country to continue our researches.

Briefly, our work was concerned with latex, the sap of the rubber tree. Le Grand had proved in a small greenhouse sort of way, that this flow could be doubled by injection, corresponding roughly to the intravenal injections of saline solution into human veins, which has already displaced transfusions among the more advanced members of the medical profession. This experiment, which would revolutionize the rubber industry, being no more to him than a proof in a large way of a hypothesis already proved in a small one.

It is not possible for me to give the name of the place we went to, because in these matters secrecy is of the utmost importance, for although this took place many years ago, observations are still being made by those who came after us.

It was forest country parts of which were so overgrown with great trees, some of them a thousand years old Le Grand said, that the sun never penetrated to the ground at their roots. The forest opened up into the glades, where natives performed a somewhat desultory form of agriculture. Growing bananas, millet, maize, sweet potatoes, pumpkins, groundnuts, and a variety of bean. The earth was fertile, and the crops invariably good; wonderfully so, considering the way in which they were neglected.

Occasionally elephants would devastate an area, but gorillas were the main trouble and were both feared and hated by the aborigines. Their depredations were not at once apparent, for with great cunning they would steal only a little at a time, and that so skilfully that unless the very pods of the beans were counted nothing would be noticed till it was time to harvest the crop.

When I say we went, it must be understood that there were three of us, for Le Grand, before going, had married a young girl. She had a knowledge of typing and shorthand and was accustomed to doing much of Le Grand's work, being one of the few who could decipher his handwriting. Helena Magrodvata was her name. She was of Greco-Russian extraction, and had fair hair, so deficient in pigmentation that it was almost white. Without her glasses she was said to be pretty, and it may be that the Professor's marriage was the logical outcome of the desire on the part of a man to possess such a woman, or it may have been another of his experiments; I have not found any notes about it, which tends to destroy this theory, and it was perhaps the only thing he never discussed with me.

We lived in a small whitewashed bungalow which had been built for us, and in due course Helena gave birth to a son. There was no particular difficulty about this, Le Grand and I being doctors of medicine, and Helena a healthy girl.

That we all lived and kept our health in that pestilential climate was due to the Professor, and we were undoubtedly the first white people to face the myriads of *Anopheles maculipennis* unperturbed by the fear of either malaria, or blackwater; both particularly malignant in those parts, even natives dying freely.

It will be the Le Grand serum which will eventually, when it comes into the market, open up vast tracts of swamp hitherto considered uninhabitable. It is possible that this was an additional reason for his wanting to go to the Congo, where he could try his experimental serums on three people of different types, sexes, and nationalities.

Not only were we well, we were in what a layman would describe as radiant health; one of the three serums he used having tonic properties of the most powerful quality.

The baby throve, putting on weight daily, and Helena was enraptured by it. Motherhood occupied her to such an extent that she did no other work, except the weekly report, which was urgent.

The Professor's interest in the infant appeared to be more academic than paternal, though when it died he did show signs of emotion. We were out together, measuring and weighing latex, when a native runner reached us with the news that the child had been bitten by a snake. Returning to the house we found the baby dead, and Helena on the verge of madness. She was inconsolable, and could not be left alone. Even Le Grand saw this after her first attempt at suicide. The interference this caused in our routine was considerable. For since we were working different sections of the forest, and the field and office work were inextricably mixed, neither of us could entirely take over the other's operations. However, the delay was not serious and our experiments proceeded. We took turns to go out to our respective areas, the Professor going one day, and I the next.

About a month later as we were eating our breakfast, the news came in that a gorilla had been trapped; and leaving Helena, who was in bed, we set off to see it.

The distance was not great, and we soon reached the native land where it had been caught. The trap, an enormous affair like a cage of logs, tied together with wire and rawhide strips, stood among the maize plants which had screened it but which were now tramped down by the natives who surrounded their prize. It had been baited with a variety of banana, of which these animals are inordinately fond. Already the gorilla was severely wounded in many places and bleeding profusely; this torturing being less a pastime than a religious rite among these people. They believe that, by so doing, they exorcise the devil which possesses it, and reduce, for a time at any rate, the depredations of its fellows.

Forcing our way through the crowd we approached the cage. The gorilla was roaring with rage and pain. It was a female, heavy in young; a quick look sufficed to show us that. A further examination convinced us both that the event was almost due, and it was then that Le Grand got his idea.

" 'Arry," he said, for in all the years of our association, and despite his wide knowledge of English literature, the aspirates of our language continued to escape him.

" 'Arry, I am going to 'ave that young one, she can't live long."

This was evident, a spear having pierced her right lung.

"Go quickly back, and bring my instruments, and chloroform. I will stop this spectacle," he added, using the word in its French sense.

That was how Congo, as we called him later, came to be born. Le Grand succeeded in getting the natives to make their prisoner fast, and by the time I got back, she was spread-eagled and lay gnashing her teeth with rage. To tie a gorilla down is something of a feat, but to enter the cage where she is tied is a thing I have done only once, and never propose to do again. The strength of these animals is phenomenal. They can take and twist the barrel of a rifle more easily than we can bend a pin.

She lay there grinning up at us, blood and saliva running down her face. Her great canine teeth were bared like those of a snarling dog as she let out yell after yell. The pupils of her eyes enormously dilated under the heavy brows.

I had seen that look before, on the face of a homicidal lunatic, one who had killed several men. It was a mixture of ferocity and cunning. One felt that though she had struggled mightily she had not yet put forth her supreme endeavor. This she did, when we got in. The whole cage rocked with her efforts, the mighty muscles of her swollen belly stood out like cords, and the milk spurted from her breasts. For a moment I thought she would break her bonds; had she done so it would not have taken long to break us, literally, into small shreds. I had imagined till that moment that I was hardened to anything, for I had

seen many horrible sights; but that colossal animal lying
there, chattering and coughing with rage, covered with
blood, upset me. She had a man's arm beside her. We had
come too late to treat him, and he had died. He would
have in any case, for, coming too near, his arm had been
torn from its socket as a branch might be plucked from a
tree. It was not the neatly amputated limb to which one
gets accustomed, but a gory lump; and Le Grand, in his
white coat, with his instruments in hand, was as calm as if
he were about to examine a bacillus through a microscope.

I do not believe his heart accelerated, or that he even
contemplated the possibility of disaster. To him this enormous anthropoid ape was a scientific problem, but I felt
otherwise. Perhaps, even then, I knew that evil would
come of this unnatural thing.

In the pursuit of scientific truth I have seen many
strange sights, but never one to equal a Cesarian operation
on a wounded gorilla in the heart of the Congo jungle.

I should hesitate to say how much chloroform we used;
some was spilt of course, but there was not much left in a
half-liter bottle when we had done. Needless to say, we put
her out of her agony. She never woke from that sleep. The
baby gorilla was wrapped up and given to one of our half-
trained dressers; we had established a sort of clinic at our
station. The Professor was bending over the dead mother,
tape measure in hand, while I did some rough dissection
before the rigor mortis set in, when to my astonishment on
turning round I saw Helena with the baby gorilla at her
breast.

The exact sequence of the preceding events I can only
guess at. I think when she got up she sought us, and coming upon the native holding the young ape, its crumpled
face so like a baby's, she took it from him instinctively.
This was the more likely as Solomon, that was his name,
had acted as nurse to her own son, so the association of
ideas would have been complete, and the gorilla, much
stronger than a human child, had clutched at her. Anyhow,
by the time I saw her it was done.

"Look," I said to the Professor, as he stood up with a
detached muscle in his hand.

"So," he said, "she has taken him."

What his idea had been I do not know. Had he performed that astonishing operation out of mere curiosity? That I doubt. Had he meant to foster the child—I keep calling him that—on to a native woman? Or had it been his intention to kill it, and preserve it as a specimen; one more to be added to his already famous collection?

And did Helena know what she had done? Again, what did we know of Helena, with her mixed blood, her strong instincts, and her veins full of experimental serums? It was a problem that could be dealt with later, Le Grand must have thought.

"Take her back," he said, "and send me some bottles." We had a storeroom full of them for specimens. "And spirits," he shouted after us as we left him.

When he came back, the sun was setting, and Helena had spoken once. "He is mine," she'd said.

That is how we returned to Brussels a year later. A Professor, his assistant, his wife and her child. For that she insisted on. It was not a gorilla, but a child, and it was dressed as a child. Only by using the great influence we had did we succeed in getting a state room for them; the shipping company maintaining that it was an animal, whereat Helena became livid. She took her meals in the cabin, for it was very noisy and screamed loudly if she left it.

It is hard to describe the voyage, particularly in view of subsequent events. Helena called it Baby. The Professor did sometimes, while as far as was possible I never referred to it at all. If she had kept it as a pet it would have been different, but it slept in her bed, Le Grand and I sharing the next cabin. At that time Helena must have been twenty. The next eight years I skip. There are some things one cannot write about.

Our work, the Professor's and my own, was successful beyond our wildest dreams. Of our life together with that "thing," now nearly nine, I will say nothing. I have already said that Helena was beautiful, the Professor no longer young, and at times absentminded; while I am in no way differently constituted from other men. One thing I knew however, that it hated us both; and already it was much stronger than a man.

How can I tell of it? Dressed up like a boy, in a sailor suit, with socks and shoes, eating at table with us, its face like that of an old man. It still slept in the same room as Helena, and the Professor in the dressing room adjoining. It had a brass bed with sheets and blankets in a corner. If it had been a child such a thing would not have been permissible, but with the inconsistency of women Helena at those times chose to regard it as other women might a dog. But it, "he," was not a dog. Congo in his loves and hates was a primitive man; for if by heredity he was an anthropoid ape, by the environment Helena forced upon him he had made a jump from one geological era to another, and mentally must have corresponded to the Neanderthal man at least. And he was in love with Helena.

I employ the term "in love" advisedly. That he should love her was natural, since she was his foster-mother and had reared him, but it went far beyond this. His precocity may have been partially due to his feeding, which had always been the same as our own, much richer in concentrated proteins than his natural diet would have been; but it was an ugly business. Superficially his attitude toward Helena was that of an affectionate child. He clung to her hand, held her skirts, climbed onto her knee, and putting his arms about her neck would kiss her lips with his mouth. The rest was only to be seen in his eyes when he thought himself unobserved; also there were times when, I am convinced, he was testing his strength. He did not do this by breaking things, he had got over that in his early childhood, he did it by moving them. I caught him one day with a trunk full of clothes above his head, he was holding it with both hands raised. Out of curiosity I noticed its weight on the station scales, seventy-five kilograms exactly. He held it as easily as a man would a parcel. We kept accurate records about him; his chest at that time was fifty-four inches, his height four feet eleven, his weight a hundred and eighty pounds in English measures. He is much bigger now.

They said it was an accident, though at first they had

tried to implicate me. The motive they said was jealousy, both of his wife, and his position in the scientific world, which they were kind enough to say I rivalled. Fortunately I was able to prove that at the time I was away lecturing, or nothing would have saved me, especially when they found he had made me his sole trustee, and had left me all his books, specimens, and manuscripts. So not only did I lose a friend, but was nearly tried for murder.

That Helena should marry me was inevitable; already for some time—but why go into that? Could any man have lived in that house, under those strange conditions, and not have behaved as I did? I doubt it. And could Helena have done without me for company while poor Le Grand was alive or as a buffer between the world and her Congo after his death? Again I doubt it. Or could I, having known and loved Helena for years? But she was mad about one thing. That ape. Nothing, not even her love for me, would part her from him.

Le Grand had fallen from a window. The flat we shared was high up on the fifth floor. He had a water can in his hand when he fell. A hundred times a day I saw it. The dear old man, for he had aged rapidly, poking at the leaf mould in his window box with a curious finger. The stealthy approach, for Congo could move as quietly as a cat and the flat was heavily carpeted. The two grasping hands, the heave, the scream, the crash.

And I am certain that Helena guesses, but neither of us dares say a word. She because of her love for Congo, I because of my desire for her. But subconsciously she knows it, and fears for me. She never leaves us alone together now; yet she is in a way defeating her own ends, for I have thought of a way to poison him, somewhat subtly. To do it with arsenic or some such stuff would lay me open to exposure, Helena's knowledge of medicine being considerable. Although legally she would have no redress, morally she would regard me as the murderer of her son. I shall use albumen; 5 C.C. should be enough.

But it is a dangerous game, one in which the time factor will play a leading part. As far as possible I go armed, using as an excuse the unrest in the rougher quarters of the

town to which my work often takes me. She says, "Surely
that pistol must be uncomfortable in your pocket, and why
carry it in the house? It spoils your clothes." It is a .32
Browning; and though I am doubtful about the stopping
power of those small bullets, I persist. Today I feel that a
crisis is upon me; so I am writing this. It is all too terrible,
and my hands are tied by my passion, but someone must
know. She, poor child, says, "He loves me like a son."

I have left the book I am working on, to write this. I only
hope

DIP IN THE POOL
Roald Dahl

ON THE MORNING OF THE THIRD DAY THE SEA CALMED. EVEN
the most delicate passengers—those who had not been seen
around the ship since sailing time—emerged from their
cabins and crept up onto the sundeck where the deck steward gave them chairs and tucked rugs around their legs and
left them lying in rows, their faces upturned to the pale, almost heatless January sun.

It had been moderately rough the first two days, and this
sudden calm and the sense of comfort that it brought cre-
ated a more genial atmosphere over the whole ship. By the
time evening came, the passengers, with twelve hours of
good weather behind them, were beginning to feel
confident, and at eight o'clock that night the main dining
room was filled with people eating and drinking with the
assured, complacent air of seasoned sailors.

The meal was not half over when the passengers became
aware, by a slight friction between their bodies and the
seats of their chairs, that the big ship had actually started
rolling again. It was very gentle at first, just a slow, lazy
leaning to one side, then to the other, but it was enough to

cause a subtle, immediate change of mood over the whole
room. A few of the passengers glanced up from their food,
hesitating, waiting, almost listening for the next roll, smiling nervously, little secret glimmers of apprehension in their
eyes. Some were completely unruffled, some were openly
smug, a number of the smug ones making jokes about food
and weather in order to torture the few who were beginning
to suffer. The movement of the ship then became rapidly
more and more violent, and only five or six minutes after
the first roll had been noticed, she was swinging heavily
from side to side, the passengers bracing themselves in
their chairs, leaning against the pull as in a car cornering.

At last the really bad roll came, and Mr. William Botibol, sitting at the purser's table, saw his plate of poached
turbot with hollandaise sauce sliding suddenly away from
under his fork. There was a flutter of excitement, everybody reaching for plates and wineglasses. Mrs. Renshaw,
seated at the purser's right, gave a little scream and
clutched that gentleman's arm.

"Going to be a dirty night," the purser said, looking at
Mrs. Renshaw. "I think it's blowing up for a very dirty
night." There was just the faintest suggestion of relish in
the way he said it.

A steward came hurrying up and sprinkled water on the
table cloth between the plates. The excitement subsided.
Most of the passengers continued with their meal. A small
number, including Mrs. Renshaw, got carefully to their
feet and threaded their ways with a kind of concealed haste
between the tables and through the doorway.

"Well," the purser said, "there she goes." He glanced
around with approval at the remainder of his flock who
were sitting quiet, looking complacent, their faces
reflecting openly that extraordinary pride that travellers
seem to take in being recognized as "good sailors."

When the eating was finished and the coffee had been
served, Mr. Botibol, who had been unusually grave and
thoughtful since the rolling started, suddenly stood up and
carried his cup of coffee around to Mrs. Renshaw's vacant
place, next to the purser. He seated himself in her chair,
then immediately leaned over and began to whisper urgent-

ly in the purser's ear. "Excuse me," he said, "but could you tell me something please?"

The purser, small and fat and red, bent forward to listen. "What's the trouble, Mr. Botibol?"

"What I want to know is this." The man's face was anxious and the purser was watching it. "What I want to know is will the captain already have made his estimate on the day's run—you know, for the auction pool? I mean before it began to get rough like this?"

The purser, who had prepared himself to receive a personal confidence, smiled and leaned back in his seat to relax his full belly. "I should say so—yes," he answered. He didn't bother to whisper his reply, although automatically he lowered his voice, as one does when answering a whisper.

"About how long ago do you think he did it?"

"Some time this afternoon. He usually does it in the afternoon."

"About what time?"

"Oh, I don't know. Around four o'clock I should guess."

"Now tell me another thing. How does the captain decide which number it shall be? Does he take a lot of trouble over that?"

The purser looked at the anxious frowning face of Mr. Botibol and he smiled, knowing quite well what the man was driving at. "Well, you see, the captain has a little conference with the navigating officer, and they study the weather and a lot of other things, and then they make their estimate."

Mr. Botibol nodded, pondering this answer for a moment. Then he said, "Do you think the captain knew there was bad weather coming today?"

"I couldn't tell you," the purser replied. He was looking into the small black eyes of the other man, seeing the two single little sparks of excitement dancing in their centers. "I really couldn't tell you, Mr. Botibol. I wouldn't know."

"If this gets any worse it might be worth buying some of the low numbers. What do you think?" The whispering was more urgent, more anxious now.

"Perhaps it will," the purser said. "I doubt the old man allowed for a really rough night. It was pretty calm this afternoon when he made his estimate."

The others at the table had become silent and were trying to hear, watching the purser with that intent, half-cocked listening look that you can see also at the race track when they are trying to overhear a trainer talking about his chance: the slightly open lips, the upstretched eyebrows, the head forward and cocked a little to one side —that desperately straining, half-hypnotized, listening look that comes to all of them when they are hearing something straight from the horse's mouth.

"Now suppose *you* were allowed to buy a number, which one would *you* choose today?" Mr. Botibol whispered.

"I don't know what the range is yet," the purser patiently answered. "They don't announce the range till the auction starts after dinner. And I'm really not very good at it anyway. I'm only the purser, you know."

At that point Mr. Botibol stood up. "Excuse me, all," he said, and he walked carefully away over the swaying floor between the other tables, and twice he had to catch hold of the back of a chair to steady himself against the ship's roll.

"The sundeck, please," he said to the elevator man.

The wind caught him full in the face as he stepped out onto the open deck. He staggered and grabbed hold of the rail and held on tight with both hands, and he stood there looking out over the darkening sea where the great waves were welling up high and white horses were riding against the wind with plumes of spray behind them as they went.

"Pretty bad out there, wasn't it?" the elevator man said on the way down.

Mr. Botibol was combing his hair back into place with a small red comb. "Do you think we've slackened speed at all on account of the weather?" he asked.

"Oh, my word yes, sir. We slacked off considerable since this started. You got to slacken off speed in weather like this or you'll be throwing the passengers all over the ship."

Down in the smoking room people were already gathering for the auction. They were grouping themselves politely around the various tables, the men a little stiff in their dinner jackets, a little pink and overshaved and stiff beside their cool, white-armed woman. Mr. Botibol took a chair close to the auctioneer's table. He crossed his legs, folded his arms, and settled himself in his seat with the rather desperate air of a man who has made a tremendous decision and refuses to be frightened.

The pool, he was telling himself, would probably be around seven thousand dollars. That was almost exactly what it had been the last two days with the numbers selling for between three and four hundred apiece. Being a British ship they did it in pounds, but he liked to do his thinking in his own currency. Seven thousand dollars was plenty of money. My goodness yes! And what he would do, he would get them to pay him in hundred-dollar bills and he would take it ashore in the inside pocket of his jacket. No problem there. And right away, yes right away, he would buy a Lincoln convertible. He would pick it up on the way from the ship and drive it home just for the pleasure of seeing Ethel's face when she came out the front door and looked at it. Wouldn't that be something, to see Ethel's face when he glided up to the door in a brand-new pale-green Lincoln convertible! Hello, Ethel honey, he would say, speaking very causal. I just thought I'd get you a little present. I saw it in the window as I went by, so I thought of you and how you were always wanting one. You like it, honey? he would say. You like the color? And then he would watch her face.

The auctioneer was standing up behind his table now. "Ladies and gentlemen!" he shouted. "The captain has estimated the day's run, ending midday tomorrow, at five hundred and fifteen miles. As usual we will take the ten numbers on either side of it to make up the range. That makes it five hundred and five to five hundred and twenty-five. And of course for those who think the true figure will be still farther away, there'll be 'low field' and 'high field' sold separately as well. Now, we'll draw the first number out of the hat . . . here we are . . . five hundred and twelve?"

The room became quiet. The people sat still in their

chairs, all eyes watching the auctioneer. There was a certain tension in the air, and as the bids got higher, the tension grew. This wasn't a game or a joke; you could be sure of that by the way one man would look across at another who had raised his bid—smiling perhaps, but only the lips smiling, the eyes bright and absolutely cold.

Number five hundred and twelve was knocked down for one hundred and ten pounds. The next three or four numbers fetched roughly the same amount.

The ship was rolling heavily, and each time she went over, the wooden panelling on the walls creaked as if it were going to split. The passengers held on to the arms of their chairs, concentrating upon the auction.

"Low field!" the auctioneer called out. "The next number is low field."

Mr. Botibol sat up very straight and tense. He would wait, he had decided, until the others had finished bidding, then he would jump in and make the last bid. He had figured that there must be at least five hundred dollars in his account at the bank at home, probably nearer six. That was about two hundred pounds—over two hundred. This ticket wouldn't fetch more than that.

"As you all know," the auctioneer was saying, "low field covers every number *below* the smallest number in the range, in this case every number below five hundred and five. So, if you think this ship is going to cover less than five hundred and five miles in the twenty-four hours ending at noon tomorrow, you better get in and buy this number. So what am I bid?"

It went clear up to one hundred and thirty pounds. Others besides Mr. Botibol seemed to have noticed that the weather was rough. One hundred and forty . . . fifty. . . . There it stopped. The auctioneer raised his hammer.

"Going at one hundred and fifty . . ."

"Sixty!" Mr. Botibol called, and every face in the room turned and looked at him.

"Seventy!"

"Eighty!" Mr. Botibol called.

"Ninety!"

"Two hundred!" Mr. Botibol called. He wasn't stopping now—not for anyone.

There was a pause.

"Any advance on two hundred pounds?"

Sit still, he told himself. Sit absolutely still and don't look up. It's unlucky to look up. Hold your breath. No one's going to bid you up so long as you hold your breath.

"Going for two hundred pounds . . ." The auctioneer had a pink bald head and there were little beads of sweat sparkling on top of it. "Going . . ." Mr. Botibol held his breath. "Going . . . Gone!" The man banged the hammer on the table. Mr. Botibol wrote out a check and handed it to the auctioneer's assistant, then he settled back in his chair to wait for the finish. He did not want to go to bed before he knew how much there was in the pool.

They added it up after the last number had been sold and it came to twenty-one hundred-odd pounds. That was around six thousand dollars. Ninety percent to go to the winner, ten percent to seamen's charities. Ninety percent of six thousand was five thousand four hundred. Well— that was enough. He could buy the Lincoln convertible and there would be something left over, too. With this gratifying thought he went off, happy and excited, to his cabin.

When Mr. Botibol awoke the next morning he lay quite still for several minutes with his eyes shut, listening for the sound of the gale, waiting for the roll of the ship. There was no sound of any gale and the ship was not rolling. He jumped up and peered out of the porthole. The sea—Oh Jesus God—was smooth as glass, the great ship was moving through it fast, obviously making up for time lost during the night. Mr. Botibol turned away and sat slowly down on the edge of his bunk. A fine electricity of fear was beginning to prickle under the skin of his stomach. He hadn't a hope now. One of the higher numbers was certain to win it after this.

"Oh my God," he said aloud. "What shall I do?"

"What, for example, would Ethel say? It was simply not possible to tell her that he had spent almost all of their two years' savings on a ticket in the ship's pool. Nor was it pos-

sible to keep the matter secret. To do that he would have to
tell her to stop drawing checks. And what about the
monthly installments on the television set and *Encyclo-
paedia Britannica?* Already he could see the anger and
contempt in the woman's eyes, the blue becoming gray and
the eyes themselves narrowing as they always did when
there was anger in them.

"Oh my God. What *shall* I do?"

There was no point in pretending that he had the slightest chance now—not unless the goddam ship started to
go backward. They'd have to put her in reverse and go full
speed astern and keep right on going if he was to have any
chance of winning it now. Well, maybe he should ask the
captain to do just that. Offer him ten percent of the profits.
Offer him more if he wanted it. Mr. Botibol started to gig-
gle. Then very suddenly he stopped, his eyes and mouth
both opening wide in a kind of shocked surprise. For it
was at this moment that the idea came. It hit him hard and
quick, and he jumped up from his bed, terribly excited, ran
over to the porthole and looked out again. Well, he
thought, why not? Why ever not? The sea was calm and he
wouldn't have any trouble keeping afloat until they picked
him up. He had a vague feeling that someone had done
this thing before, but that didn't prevent him from doing it
again. The ship would have to stop and lower a boat, and
the boat would have to go back maybe a half a mile to get
him, and then it would have to return to the ship and be
hoisted back on board. It would take at least an hour, the
whole thing. An hour was about thirty miles. It would
knock thirty miles off the day's run. That would do it.
"Low field" would be sure to win it then. Just so long as he
made certain someone saw him falling over; but that would
be simple to arrange. And he'd better wear light clothes,
something easy to swim in. Sports clothes, that was it. He
would dress as though he were going up to play some deck
tennis—just a shirt and a pair of shorts and tennis shoes.
And leave his watch behind. What was the time? Nine-
fifteen. The sooner the better, then. Do it now and get it

over with. Have to do it soon, because the time limit was midday.

Mr. Botibol was both frightened and excited when he stepped out onto the sundeck in his sports clothes. His small body was wide at the hips, tapering upward to extremely narrow sloping shoulders, so that it resembled, in shape at any rate, a bollard. His white skinny legs were covered with black hairs, and he came cautiously out on deck, treading softly in his tennis shoes. Nervously he looked around him. There was only one other person in sight, an elderly woman with very thick ankles and immense buttocks who was leaning over the rail staring at the sea. She was wearing a coat of Persian lamb and the collar was turned up so Mr. Botibol couldn't see her face.

He stood still, examining her carefully from a distance. Yes, he told himself, she would probably do. She would probably give the alarm just as quickly as anyone else. But wait one minute, take your time, William Botibol, take your time. Remember what you told yourself a few minutes ago in the cabin when you were changing? You remember that?

The thought of leaping off a ship into the ocean a thousand miles from the nearest land had made Mr. Botibol—a cautious man at the best of times—unusually advertent. He was by no means satisfied yet that this woman he saw before him was *absolutely certain* to give the alarm when he made his jump. In his opinion there were two possible reasons why she might fail him. Firstly, she might be deaf and blind. It was not very probable, but on the other hand it *might* be so, and why take a chance? All he had to do was check it by talking to her for a moment beforehand. Secondly—and this will demonstrate how suspicious the mind of a man can become when it is working through self-preservation and fear—secondly, it had occurred to him that the woman might herself be the owner of one of the high numbers in the pool and as such would have a sound financial reason for not wishing to stop the ship. Mr. Botibol recalled that people had killed their fellows for far less than six thousand dollars. It was happening every day in the

newspapers. So why take a chance on that either? Check
on it first. Be sure of your facts. Find out about it by a little polite conversation. Then, provided that the woman appeared also to be a pleasant, kindly human being, the thing
was a cinch and he could leap overboard with a light heart.

Mr. Botibol advanced casually toward the woman and
took up a position beside her, leaning on the rail. "Hullo,"
he said pleasantly.

She turned and smiled at him, a surprisingly lovely, almost a beautiful smile, although the face itself was very
plain. "Hullo," she answered him.

Check, Mr. Botibol told himself, on the first question.
She is neither blind nor deaf. "Tell me," he said, coming
straight to the point, "what did you think of the auction
last night?"

"Auction?" she asked, frowning. "Auction? What auction?"

"You know, that silly old thing they have in the lounge
after dinner, selling numbers on the ship's daily run. I just
wondered what you thought about it."

She shook her head, and again she smiled, a sweet and
pleasant smile that had in it perhaps the trace of an apolo-
gy. "I'm very lazy," she said. "I always go to bed early. I
have my dinner in bed. It's so restful to have dinner in
bed."

Mr. Botibol smiled back at her and began to edge away.
"Got to go and get my exercise now," he said. "Never miss
my exercise in the morning. It was nice seeing you. Very
nice seeing you . . ." He retreated about ten paces, and
the woman let him go without looking around.

Everything was now in order. The sea was calm, he was
lightly dressed for swimming, there were almost certainly
no man-eating sharks in this part of the Atlantic, and there
was this pleasant kindly old woman to give the alarm. It
was a question now only of whether the ship would be de-
layed long enough to swing the balance in his favor. Almost certainly it would. In any event, he could do a little
to help in that direction himself. He could make a few
difficulties about getting hauled up into the lifeboat. Swim

around a bit, back away from them surreptitiously as they
tried to come up close to fish him out. Every minute, every
second gained would help him win. He began to move forward again to the rail, but now a new fear assailed him.
Would he get caught in the propeller? He had heard about
that happening to persons falling off the sides of big ships.
But then, he wasn't going to fall, he was going to jump,
and that was a very different thing. Provided he jumped
out far enough he would be sure to clear the propeller.

Mr. Botibol advanced slowly to a position at the rail
about twenty yards away from the woman. She wasn't looking at him now. So much the better. He didn't want her
watching him as he jumped off. So long as no one was
watching he would be able to say afterward that he had
slipped and fallen by accident. He peered over the side of
the ship. It was a long, long drop. Come to think of it now,
he might easily hurt himself badly if he hit the water flat.
Wasn't there someone who once split his stomach open
that way, doing a belly flop from the high dive? He must
jump straight and land feet first. Go in like a knife. Yes sir.
The water seemed cold and deep and gray and it made him
shiver to look at it. But it was now or never. Be a man,
William Botibol, be a man. All right then . . . now . . .
here goes . . .

He climbed up onto the wide wooden toprail, stood
there poised, balancing for three terrifying seconds, then
he leaped—he leaped up and out as far as he could go and
at the same time he shouted *"Help!"*

"Help! Help!" he shouted as he fell. Then he hit the
water and went under.

When the first shout for help sounded, the woman who
was leaning on the rail started up and gave a little jump of
surprise. She looked around quickly and saw sailing past
her through the air this small man dressed in white shorts
and tennis shoes, spread-eagled and shouting as he went.
For a moment she looked as though she weren't quite sure
what she ought to do: throw a life belt, run away and give
the alarm, or simply turn and yell. She drew back a pace

from the rail and swung half around facing up to the bridge, and for this brief moment she remained motionless, tense, undecided. Then almost at once she seemed to relax, and she leaned forward far over the rail, staring at the water where it was turbulent in the ship's wake. Soon a tiny round black head appeared in the foam, an arm was raised about it, once, twice, vigorously waving, and a small faraway voice was heard calling something that was difficult to understand. The woman leaned still farther over the rail, trying to keep the little bobbing black speck in sight, but soon, so very soon, it was such a long way away that she couldn't even be sure it was there at all.

After a while another woman came out on deck. This one was bony and angular, and she wore horn-rimmed spectacles. She spotted the first woman and walked over to her, treading the deck in the deliberate, military fashion of all spinsters.

"So *there* you are," she said.

The woman with the fat ankles turned and looked at her, but said nothing.

"I've been searching for you," the bony one continued. "Searching all over."

"It's very odd," the woman with the fat ankles said. "A man dived overboard just now, with his clothes on."

"Nonsense!"

"Oh, yes. He said he wanted to get some exercise and he dived in and didn't even bother to take his clothes off."

"You better come down now," the bony woman said. Her mouth had suddenly become firm, her whole face sharp and alert, and she spoke less kindly than before. "And don't you ever go wandering about on deck alone like this again. You know quite well you're meant to wait for me."

"Yes, Maggie," the woman with the fat ankles answered, and again she smiled, a tender, trusting smile, and she took the hand of the other one and allowed herself to be led away across the deck.

"Such a nice man," she said. "He waved to me."

I DO NOT HEAR YOU, SIR

Avram Davidson

BLOODGOOD BIXBEE KNEW NOTHING ABOUT ART, BUT HE knew what he didn't like: What he didn't like, he said—loudly and with much profane redundancy—was Bein Played For A Sucker . . . See?

Milo Anderson saw, all right; he knew he should never have sold Bixbee the unauthenticated Wilson Peale, anymore than he should have collected in advance the five percent of the contract which he could never negotiate. But there were so few people left in the capital whom he could still expect to swindle . . . and he needed the money. He had counted too much on Bixbee's not being able to admit participation in an illegal deal, and it certainly wasn't the moral aspect of not telling the rich lumberman about the cloud on the picture's title which worried him. In fact, nothing about Bixbee had worried him at the time—for who, back in Qualliupp, Washington, would know a Wilson Peale from a citron peel?—all that concerned him had been getting the check to the bank in time. And then to the phone. . . .

Checks, checks, telephones, telephones, and . . .

Damn them all, with their greedy open hands and yapping mouths.

> Big crooks have littler crooks to bite 'um,
> And so on down, ad infinitum.

Wasn't Bloodgood Bixbee a crook, stealing lumber rights and ravishing the forests with a ruthless hand? Sure he was. And then following the classic pattern of trying to set himself up as a man of culture, with Genuine Oil Paintings on his walls. How the *Hell* did he find out, anyway? Was it possible that even Qualliupp had in it someone like Edmond Hart Ransome, from whom Milo had gotten the picture? No, impossible. The whole State of Washington was too new to interest old E.H.R., who seldom concerned himself with anything later than the end of the 1700's.

Anderson ran over in his mind the list of those with whom he had done business. Some one of them—there had to be at least *one*—would be in a mood to help him now, to advance money against future cooperation.

He dialed an unlisted number, tried to swallow. A man's voice, very quiet and cautious: "Yes?"

"Ovlomov?" He must not seem too—

"Who is this?" the voice inquired. A man with whom Mr. Ovlomov had done business? Didn't he know that Mr. Ovlomov had returned only that day to his homeland? He should follow the newspapers—No, no—he, the one speaking, was not interested in Ovlomov's contacts. Nor would it be of any use to call again: the number was being discontinued: Ovlomov was indiscreet.

So that way—the way of being a tenth-rate spy pretending to be a third-rate one—was out, and he was no closer to being clear of his snarl of checks and phone calls: people he was blackmailing (but only able to get small sums from), people who were blackmailing *him* (and getting large sums). For a while he had had an easy stretch, living at old Ransome's place.

The lease was up in a few days—another problem.

It wasn't as if the painting wasn't his; Ransome had left it to him, it was clear enough in his will. That was the devilish part of it—before simply stating "and all the rest of my property now located in my apartment," the old man had "left" him, had specifically named, every single article Milo had stolen from him. He had *known.* "And this bequest I make for a reason well known to my secretary, the said Milo Anderson." Rubbing it in. *Always* rubbing it in. *"Fast horses and slow women, eh, Mr. Anderson?"* That sort of thing.

Perhaps it would have been better not to have meddled with the old man's medicine bottles—but it was *so* easy—and so soon after the doctor had called; no trouble about a death certificate. . . . *All the rest of my property . . . for a reason well known to the said Milo Anderson.*

But little enough property was left in the apartment by now.

By now everything was coming all at once. Bloodgood
Bixbee wanting his money back and raving raw head and
bloody bones if he didn't get it. Big Patsy the bookmaker
wanting the markers to be made good, wanting it right
away, not threatening but promising. And Mrs. Pritchard,
her voice like half-melted margarine: "Carried you on the
books a long time, Milo—been good to you—we all've
been good to you. Now we have to get the money because
the Syndicate goes over the books tomorrow, and you
know what *that* means, Milo."

And he knew, oh, he *knew* all right. Even before the
phone rang and the voice—an ordinary coarse unlettered
unviolent sort of voice, saying its say as the cabbie might
ask Where To or the laundryman announce the bill—Anderson: Get it ready, get the money ready, we'll pick it up
(by now the voice a bit bored with so many routine calls)
as soon after midnight as we get around there. . . .

Milo Anderson's eye ran hopelessly around the apartment. Over the mantelpiece (or over where the marble had
been before he'd sold it) was the faded place where the
alleged Wilson Peale had hung before going to take its
place over the silent hi-fi set in the Bloodgood Bixbee place
in Qualliupp (who'd bother with hi-fi when the TV offered
such quality fare?). The cabinet of old coins had stood
over there—the Pine Tree shillings, the "York" pieces, half-
reales, the dismes: all sold by now, and sold well, but the
money long ago (it seemed long ago) spent . . . Big Patsy,
Mrs. Pritchard, and all the others . . . Edward Hart Ransome's place had been stuffed with the treasures of the late
1700's, but almost everything had been sold or pawned by
now except for a few pieces of essential furniture. These
had been already priced and would bring only a fraction of
what was needed.

Milo Anderson was not more fearful than most men,
perhaps he was a degree less fearful. But there were too
many things piling up just now. Everybody was putting the
screws on him and there was nobody he could squeeze in
turn—not *now*—not *tonight*. . . . Like a hungry man
who opens and reopens icebox and pantry: there must be
some food left, only let me look once more: Milo roamed

the shadowy apartment, looking and peering and hoping and fearing, something to sell, something overlooked, *something* . . .

With sweat cold on his back and with kneecaps articulating far from firmly, he pawed among the discards the dealers had left. Bellows, wood-carders, trivets ("Three for a quarter on the Boston Post Road," the dealer said.), applecorers and nutmeg graters, new model spinningwheels . . . and *this* damned thing. Whatever *it* was. The dealer had simply laughed. Milo was about to kick it. He groaned, sighed heavily, listlessly began to examine it.

Basic design was a cabinet, smallish box, done—he peered closer—in curly cherrywood, a favorite wood of the period. It stood on four legs and on *one* side was a little wheel and on the *other* side, just sticking out, was a curved copper or brass . . . funnel, was it? He twisted the metal horn, it moved under pressure. He turned the wheel. Nothing happened, and this was, of course, wrong: for no Colonial craftsman would have spent time making a device which didn't *do* anything. He spun the wheel again, and a bell tinkled inside.

Well, yes—a box had to have an inside. Why hadn't he looked inside? People (he pushed a stubborn peg) were always hiding money inside of . . . There. The panel slid open easily enough. The bell tinkled again, a tiny silver bell on a silver loop in an upper corner. A small black horn (calf? bison?) hung on a thong. Copper wires led from the small end of the horn, and parchment, like a tiny drumhead, covered the wide end. Wedged firmly behind a glass panel were two glass jars lined with metal foil.

The thing to do was to get a hammer and—the bell rang a third time. Death, he thought, was waiting, and here *he* was, playing with an antique toy. He seized the horn, was about to tear it loose, then he put it to his ear instead. At once he dropped it and jumped.

"Your conversant, Sir?" That was what the horn had said in his ear. Or was it, "You're conversant . . . ?" What was the apparatus supposed to be, a music box with vox humana, a primitive phonograph, a . . . No, if it resembled any piece of equipment he was familiar with, it was the telephone. Without stopping to rationalize his action in turning eagerly to anything which could divert him from his trouble, he thought, Let's see: Buffalo horn to ear, speak into . . . mm . . . copper tube (funnel, trumpet) on outside. Feeling a bit foolish, he said—what else *could* he say but: "Hello?"

The odd voice in his ear repeated what it had said before. Milo asked, "Conversant with *what?*"

"With *whom,* Sir," the voice corrected him; and then, as he remained baffled and silent: "I do not hear you, Sir. Pray consult the compendium, Sir, for the cypher of the conversant desired. . . . Servant, Sir."

"Hello? Hello? Hey!" He even whistled shrilly, but there was no reply.

Putting the horn down he began pressing and poking around the box, and dislodged something from a narrow space under the shelf where the odd jars were. It was a small thin leather-bound book. He opened it. Obviously laid paper, linen-rag, age-yellowed and "foxed": brown-flecked . . . names, numbers . . . turn to the front . . .

THE COMPENDIUM OF THE
NAMES, RESIDENCES, &
CYPHERS OF THE
HONORABLE & WORTHY
PATRONS OF THE
MAGNETICKAL INTELLI-
GENCE ENGINE.

Assuming—and a crazy-mad assumption it was, but here the thing stood in front of him—assuming that the telephone, or some long-forgotten precursor of it, *had* been invented in those days . . . But how could it still be working? Or was this some quirk of a few other off-beat antiquarians like old Ransome, to have their own odd-ball Bell System? Or was he simply out of his senses and imagining it all? Oh, well. He turned the page.

EXORDIUM. *The Artificers of this Device have spared neither Pains nor Oeconomy to obtain the primest Materials and Workmanship, the Cabinetmaking being that of Mr. D. Phyfe, the Leyden-jars and other*

Magnetick Parts are the Manufactory of Dr. B. Franklin, Mr. P. Revere has fabricated the Copper and Brass, and Mr. Meyer Meyers the Pewter and Silver.

SUBMONITION. *The Cypher of each Patron is listed Alphabetickally. Spin the Wheel and on perceiving the Tintinnabulation of the Bell, Inform the Engineer of the Cypher of the Conversant desired.* CAVEAT. *It is absolutely inhibited to tamper with the Leyden-jars.*

Still dubious, but certainly curious, so much so that he even forgot his own danger, Anderson looked through the book. Almost automatically his finger stopped at *Washington, Geo., Gent. Planter, Mt. Vernon.* He spun the wheel. The bell tinkled. He put the small horn to his ear.

"Your conversant, Sir?"

This time he was prepared. He cleared his throat and said, "Patriot 1-7-7-0."

"Your servant, Sir." Somewhere away another little bell began to tinkle.

"Say—Engineer?" Milo ventured.

"Servant, Sir."

"Um . . . what's your name?"

"There are no names, Sir."

Trrrinnggg . . . trrrinnggg . . .

"Well, uh, what *time* are you in—or where *are* you?"

"There is neither time nor place, Sir. And it is not permitted to hold nonpertinent discourse whilst the engine is in use, Sir." Trrrinnggg . . .

Suddenly the parchment crackled and a deep voice boomed from the horn: "Ah heah you, Seh!" Milo swallowed.

"Mr. *Wash*ington?" Surely not yet General in 1770.

"Yes, Seh—*and* no thanks to you, Seh! What do you mean by it, you damned horse-leecher? Sellin me these *con*founded artifized denticles—! Why, a wind-broken, bog-spavined *stal*lion couldn't get 'em comftable in his mouth!" The false teeth were heard clacking and grinding. The Patriot's voice rose. "Haven't ett a decent piece of butcher's meat in *days!* Live on syllabub and sugar-tiddy! Plague take your flimsy British crafts—give me honest Colonial works, say I!" The outraged voice rang in Milo's ear, then died away.

Mistaken for a quack dentist! Perhaps the only crime he never had committed. Milo wanted to call back, found he'd forgotten the number—the "cypher," rather—but the place where it had been was blank. He shivered. The engineer's voice responded to his signal. "What is George Washington's cypher?" Milo demanded.

"That intelligence is not available, Sir. Pray consult—"

"But it's no longer *in* the compendium!"

"Cyphers not in the compendium do not exist. . . . Your servant, Sir."

Well, so much for the Father of His Country. Anderson had discovered a hitherto-overlooked cause of the American Revolution, but a lot of good it did him. Once again, he realized his position. There was no one he could turn to —not in the present, anyway. Not knowing what else *to* do, he turned once more to the past. Spun the wheel, opened the little book.

"Your conversant, Sir?"

Printing house 1-7-7-1. . . ." Trrrinnggg . . . The voice was brisk, still retaining after all the years a trace of the Boston twang.

"We must all hang together or we shall surely hang separately. . . . What's your need, neighbor? The colonies should and will unite, but meanwhile the day's work goes on."

"Benjamin Franklin, I presume?"

"That same, my friend. Job-printing? Nice new line of chapbooks for your pleasure and instruction? Latest number of *Poor Richard's Almanack? Bay Psalm Book?* Biblical Concordance? Hey?"

"No, no . . ."

The voice dropped a notch, became confidential. "Just on hand by the last vessel to arrive in port, a French novel in three volumes . . . no? Make you a special price for *Fanny Hill!*"

"Dr. Franklin"—Milo grew anxious—"I need your help.

I appreciate—I appeal to you—a Fellow American—" he
stumbled.

The voice grew wary, then a trifle amused. "Nay, nay,
I'm too old a tomcod to be taken with such bait as that.
None of your Tory tricks. If you're working for Sir William
Johnson, now, tell him—"

"But—"

"Tell him I'm a loyal subject of the King until he proves
otherwise. I do but propose a continental union against
French Lewis, the Dons, and the savage Enjians—though
if Providence doesn't take most of these off our hands by
rum and pox—"

Milo cried, "My life's in terrible danger!"

"Sell you a nice ephemeris—you can cast your horo-
scope and thus see the hazards you must needs discounte-
nance. . . . Stove? Sell you a Franklin st——"

Of course, the cypher had vanished from the book and
from his memory. It was plain he was allowed but one call
to each name. And time was running short: it grew close
to midnight and he could expect to hear from the Syndicate about the money he owed Mrs. Pritchard—if Bloodgood Bixbee and his friends, or Big Patsy and *his* friends
didn't arrive first.

Well, no help from the Continentals: Try the Tories. Try
the line he'd first used to approach Ovlomov: spin the
wheel and hear the bell ring. ". . . Sir?"

"Slaughter 1-7-7-7. . . . Hello?"

"I hear you, Sir." Cold, this voice, and smooth as an ad-
der's skin.

"Sir Henry Hamilton? I'm a loyal subject of the King
and I have information to sell. . . ." He held his face close
to the brazen mouthpiece. By now he had no slightest
doubt but that it was all real: he would connive, he
would—

"Oh, demn the loyal subjects of the King. I buy no information; I buy *hair*, Sir! *That's* how I make rebels into
loyal subjects of the King, Sir! I buy their sculps! Have
you some'at to sell, fellow? I pay top prices to encourage
the trade—for the sculps of male Yenkees, two-pun-ten—

female Yenkees, two-pun-even—infant Yenkees and dis-
affected Injians, ten shillin."

"Help me—help me get through to where you are—Sir
Henry—I'll do—"

The Tory agent's voice grew cautionary. "Though,
mind," he said; "mind they be well-cured, for if there's one
thing I can*not* abide, d'ye hear, Sir," he said with fastidi-
ous distaste, "it's a mouldy stinking sculp. *Fah!*"

"*You* can find out how, some way, there must be a way
I can come over—"

The voice grew fainter. "*Hair;* not the whole head: just
the *haiiirrr. . . .*"

It died away altogether and while Milo watched the
name faded from the page.

One after the other he called them up. And one after
the other, though they did not know who he really was,
they knew at once that he was a rogue and a scoundrel.
He could not make them understand, could not find out
how to get from his time and place to theirs. Voices traveled
it, why not bodies? Desperately he riffled the pages of his
compendium. Another name leaped at him. *This* man
would not repulse him. He spun the wheel.

"Your conversant, Sir?"

"Tammany 1-7-8-9. And hurry!"

". . . Servant, Sir." Trrrinnggg . . .

A babble of voices . . . laughter . . . the sound of a
fiddler . . .

Milo's voice trembled. "Colonel Aaron Burr?"

The colonel's voice was soft as cream. "That same, Sir."

Lay the cards on the table. "Colonel Burr, I'm a thief, a
swindler, a blackmailer, and a traitor."

The colonel chuckled. "Ecawd, but withal an honest
knave. . . . Nay, babe, nay, my poppet, don't jump so
when I—"

"I need your help. I need it *now!*"

"Ah, not tonight, me lad. Burr might sell his soul for
gold, but he'd not move outside the door even to *save* his
soul when a pretty wench is on his knee—Why so flushed,
my sweet tapstress? Bodice tight? Let me loose it. . . .
Nay, don't slap my fingers. You know you love me. . . ."

Was there a single name left in the book? (Only a few minutes to midnight.) Yes. One.

"Your conversant, Sir?" Milo licked dry lips. "West Point 1-7-8-0." This time no silver bell tinkled. Slowly and with abrupt bursts, as if blown by gusts of wind, he heard the sound of a ruffle of drums. . . . A puff of yellow choking sulfurous smoke billowed from the coppery horn. Milo ducked his head.

"I hear you, Sir." The voice was infinitely weary, infinitely bitter.

Milo croaked, "General Benedict Arnold?" And he told the whole story. There was a silence, but he sensed the listener was still there. And finally—

"I *can* help you. Matter *can* pass the barrier of time and place. For the sake of my wounded leg at Saratoga, shattered and bloodied in the service of my native land, I will do my native land this last service." Milo babbled thanks. The bitter, weary voice spoke on. "For my treasons I received money, commissions for myself and sons, a pension for my wife. Dust, all dust and ashes . . . I ask in my will that I be buried in my Continental uniform—"

"But *me,* you said you'd help *me*—" And the clock hands almost—

"I shall do for you what I should have done for myself. My old trade, in Hartford-town, ere I turned to war, I learned—But it's too late now. I should have done it that night at West Point, before I wrote to poor André—" One of the Leyden jars shattered with a sharp crack, splitting the glass panel. He reeled from a blast of heat. Amid the dust and shards he saw a small round box.

"No!" he cried, pulling back. The clock began softly to strike the hour. An automobile drove up below, heavy feet tramped the hallway, stopped outside his door.

Without further hesitation he opened the box, thrust something into his mouth. He trembled, fell forward, grasping the wheel. The bell tinkled once. The pillbox lay to one side. "Ben. dT Arnold, Hartford," the label said. "Licensed Apotheckary."

Fists beat at the door, feet kicked it, rough voices called out.

The bell tinkled once more in the cabinet.
"Your conversant, Sir?" a voice asked faintly.
It repeated the question.
"I do not hear you, Sir," it said, at length.
"I do not hear you. . . ."

THE ARBUTUS COLLAR

Jeremiah Digges

"I REMEMBER GAFFER MORGAN AS A BIG MAN," BLOWER TOM said. "Rising six foot and broad athwartships too—though I never think of him as fat, somehow. Some men are just fat and some fat men are big. To me, a young footmaker at six dollars a week, trying to learn and still throwing my best glass back in the cullet box when I was finished muddling it, the great Shebnah Morgan was a whole lot like God Almighty, even if he was an off-Cape furriner."

Poley, the glider, had been telling them old boys about Gaffer Morgan's chastity rose, that flower of ruby glass which held clear as the waters of Shawme Pond when it was placed in the hand of a virgin, but clouded at once if the girl had been yonderly. Now, before the whistle should call them back, the lads perching on sand-kags around the glory-hole of the Sandwich glasshouse wanted old Tom to carry on the yarning about that fabulous name of Morgan.

He had a white beard, Blower Tom went on, and that made him all the more like God, and he walked like God and ate his lunch like God. The only spot where the Gaffer fell short was his quiet way. He wouldn't do hurt to a beach flea, and he had a soft, wisterly voice, and somehow God ain't that seasonable in a young man's private notions.

Ah, but they were gentlemen, the gaffers of that day, and prouder than a Truro mackerelman with a barm o'fish! The Glassmakers' Ball was the big night of the year in Sandwich, the night when the gaffers' wives come to Town Hall rigged up in the glass finery their husbands made for 'em, and each trying to outshine the rest for the prizes.

Those were the days when there was five hundred men working in this same glasshouse, and all the forty-eight pots in the upper and lower houses a-batching full. It was Sandwich then, and nobody in the trade was measuring the wages against Pittsburgh and the West, and talking strike, and going on like a Portugee parliament about conditions. It was glass then, glass and the hand, and the witching dazzlement of the articles the gaffers made; and sometimes it was the fey things they did with 'em too.

But there wasn't none of 'em could turn out the glass that Shebnah Morgan did, not one that knew the fonderly ways of it, clean from the roughing to the Craig-leithing and blue-mitering. Nobody thought of even trying to come up to the ornaments Shebnah Morgan's wife wore to the Glassmakers' Ball. Such things was fish for the fisherman. 'Twas only in the years after his wife, Maria Morgan, died, and the Gaffer quit turning out offhand pieces, that the prizing of the glass was taken up again among the rest.

We all thought Gaffer Morgan would never rally when his wife died. I've known men to look cheerly to the happiness of their wives, but I've never seen it since the way 'twas with him. And I've never seen a man so heart-shattered as he was when he lost her—though you wouldn't know it of him, I presume, if you wasn't close to the man. 'Twas by the little things, the things a stranger would pass by, that I could tell what that man's tribulation was. And if it hadn't been for his son Slade, he might have gone all to cullet.

Slade was his boy, and the pressed image of his mother. Fine, sharp face, and nervous and quick-hearted, and that was like her too. He was about fifteen when his mother died, and from that time on the lad was all the old man had to live for.

Shebnah did live for him too—more, I presume, than was good for the young feller. When the Gaffer had a word to say at all in those days—and that wasn't much oftener than a new headstone went up in the burying-ground alongside of Shawme Pond—it was like to be Slade, Slade this and Slade that.

Well, Slade Morgan was an up-bearing kind of a lad,

worth a good part of the concern his old man took in him. Though not all of it, I presume, or he might have handled his own affairs better than he did.

What I propose to say is, if Slade Morgan had steered a course as near God's own as Old Shebnah believed of him, the lad might have had better sailing orders than to marry Delly Hodges, God rest her soul!

And still, with the mold and finish Delly had, I don't suppose you could hold that mistake too hard against him. Any man would look twice at Delly, and try more times than that to get a look back from her. And many did try, and a good store got! Old Shebnah himself knew she was a veering sort of a girl, but by the time he'd grown so easy-handed with Slade that he'd clean worked to wind'ard of his own judgment, warped his mind around to thinking Slade's way. 'Twas all right if his son Slade said so. Blisters in a bubble would be all right if 'twas Slade Morgan on the other end of the blowpipe.

So, against the back of his head, Gaffer Morgan let the town know he judged Delly was a fine girl. He talked more than common, just to make certain the whole of Sandwich would know it. He passed Thankful Stocker one day on Sag-amore Road and stopped her. Thankful was a woman who could count the missing pickets in her neighbor's fence quicker'n she could mend her own, and you wouldn't find Shebnah Morgan crossing the road to her of a morn-ing when his need was no bigger than to trade a slatch of gossip.

"I knew 'twould gratify you to hear my boy Slade is marrying Delly Hodges," the Gaffer told her in his soft, low voice. "I'm the second happiest man in Sandwich today!"

"Ah, Gaffer!" Thankful answered, steeving up her best ear for more. But the Gaffer passed on with that, the smile leaving his face like the sun crossing a cloudrift, and Thankful went hurrying for her next port o' call.

Then, after the marriage of Slade and Delly, the old man went back into quiet. He was quieter than he'd ever been, and if Delly Morgan set loose a breeze into the sails of Thankful Stocker and the other town gossips two years later, you'd never have known it to talk with the Gaffer. If there was talk started when Nat Maddock come to Sandwich to take work in the glasshouse, talk of Nat and Delly Morgan, you'd never pry a word of it out of the old man.

Nat Maddock was young and incautious and without a church. And Delly, as I've mentioned, was anchor-shy from the beginning. It started gradual, and sometimes I wonder whether it was them two that really set out for each other or Slade Morgan's eternal suspicions and the galloping temper of the man, that drove them to it.

Whatever, Gaffer Morgan knew. All there was to know of it, he knew. He had the soul of Delly Morgan cleanscaled, boned and slivered while Slade was still searching for the trouble and blind-fretting over the way his wife had changed.

That's why she hated the old man so, I presume. She got to hating him out loud, and in about the same degree that she got to langifying for Nat Maddock, she got to laying her trouble to the old man—though she kept her tongue about Nat. For some reason she put it on the Gaffer for her misfortune in being haltered down to his boy.

Well, Gaffer Morgan knew women. He was willing to let her take it out on him to her heart's ease so long as she stood by of wrecking his boy's life past salvage. He never said a harsh word to Delly.

No, 'twas Slade himself that brought the flare out o' those coals. I'll never forget the day. Right here in the glasshouse, it happened. Maddock was a gatherer and Slade was a blower. Neither one of them held the rank of gaffer in the house, and when an order come for a big shipment of lamp chimneys—work that didn't want much of a hand—Maddock and young Morgan was put on it, and both of 'em working the same pot.

All of a sudden, that afternoon, Slade took the pipe from Maddock, gathered and ready for blowing the same as always, but instead of shaping out his bubble he turned and swung the pipe around on Nat Maddock. Nat must have been looking for something of the kind, for quick as that pipe come around with a mean, whining sound, he ducked. The hot glass flew off and passed over his head and slapped against the brick wall.

Looking up from his marver, Gaffer Morgan saw enough to bring him to his feet. He came running over just in time to rist the blowpipe out of Slade's hand before the boy could make another swing with it. Then the old man stood there and looked at Slade. He was breathing hard and his heavy face was wet. Slade give his father eye for eye, then turned and pointed to the pot.

"This man tried to kill me, father," he said. "Look there!"

Well, there was a crack in that pot, on the side where Slade worked, and it wasn't a new pot proving up defective, and the crack wasn't a natural breakage either. Anybody could see that the outside had been tampered with, chipped, to start the crack. It would have kept on widening, gradually, till it split open, and when it did that, it would have tossed out half a ton of the fused batch in Slade's direction.

Nat Maddock smiled.

"So you think I'd crack a pot I'm working myself, eh?" he asked Slade.

"You've been keeping out of the way of it all day," Slade said. "That's how I come to see it. And if there's killing to be done—" he made a pass to get clear of the Gaffer, who was holding him by the arm, but Shebnah kept a taut grip and a couple of other men stepped in.

Everybody in Sandwich knew what went into the swinging of that blowpipe, I presume, but nobody could pin down the pot-cracking on Nat. So a new pot was put in, and because Nat was showing himself a good steady hand at the work, the whole thing was let to pass off. Myself, I'm certain Nat done it. 'Twas taking a big chance, him working that same pot, for they've been known to spit like a sea clam. And there's no pain more terrible than the burn of fused glass. But Nat Maddock was a gaming kind of man, without a church, and willing to pay out the full slack to his luck.

Gaffer Morgan couldn't work no more that afternoon. Sam Dyer took him home. The old man was sweating like a cranberry bog and shaking all over. And in the days that come after, he was like a man set on by the black conjury. And all, of course, because he thought he saw what was coming. He'd loved Maria Morgan, but he'd known her too. He knew the flint his son was made of. Blood on Slade Morgan's hands—that's what the Gaffer saw coming, and the sight of it was more than he could bear. His own boy a murderer! All that he had left of Maria! And in the Gaffer's eyes, the mark was already on Slade. And in the Gaffer's mind at night come visions, visions he was helpless to paint out, the awful processions that guilty men see, and the end of those processions that even the guilty don't have to see.

And yet, when a man looks ahead and raises something out of the future that's worse than death to him, there's something in him won't believe it. There's a spot that chooses to be blind. The day after that ruction in the glasshouse, Shebnah Morgan busied himself to take the wind out of fate's own sails. The Glassmakers' Ball was six weeks away. He told Slade, the next day, he was going to make something for Delly to wear to the ball, something that would dazzle the town once more, the way Maria Morgan used to do with the things he made for her.

"But Delly ain't going to the ball, father," Slade said darkly.

The Gaffer made out surprised.

"You two not going to the Glassmakers' Ball, son? Why, the town will expect you—you and Delly together!"

Slade saw there was more than the wish to this. Yes, he'd *have* to be at the Glassmakers' Ball, just to bring loose tongues to moorage if for naught else.

"Nat Maddock will be there," Slade said, giving the words to his thoughts. Then he turned on the Gaffer. "If he so much as looks at Delly, by God, I'll kill him!"

Gaffer Morgan stood before his son and looked at him a long time. He shook his head and spoke slow and troubled.

"Thou shalt not kill!"

It come out of him, not like the commandment, but like a prayer, a broken, desperate kind of a prayer. It was the great Gaffer Shebnah Morgan leaning on the authority of the Almighty, calling down the workmanship of a Hand greater than his own. And Slade Morgan heard it, heard the prayer in it instead of the command, the heart-shattered prayer of a proud man who was humbled, of the old man who was his father, and he got down on his knees, that lad, and wept.

Then Shebnah laid a hand on the boy and said, "Take her to the ball, son. Take her and let her wear the little trinket I shall make for her. It will make her happy."

That's all I'm told that Gaffer Morgan said to his son. But he knew Delly was lost, lost to Slade forever, that holding to her then was like caging Will o' the Lantern all night for the morning.

That night the Gaffer got to work, and he worked late hours each night from that time on, and he come to work mornings looking the older too, for the late watches he put in.

Before many days it come to me what give him that look, though 'twas only a hunch with me. Yes, old Shebnah was putting something into that glass, something he was tearing out of his immortal soul itself. Young as I was then, that much I felt. I saw the man altering, day to day. I saw the fog heavying down, there in his eyes. I saw him parting with the thing he'd wanted to skipper within himself to the grave, and the parting that left him derelict in heart was leaving him derelict in face as well.

Now, the thing he made for his daughter-in-law was a white glass collar of trailing arbutus, as he put it. We call it the mayflower, but the old man was English and off-Cape in his talk, like most of the gaffers of that day, and trailing arbutus was his name for it.

Nobody in the world could have made that collar but Shebnah Morgan. I'd never seen glass like it before and I don't hope to see the match of it again.

It was diamond-white, not a yellow cast in it, and it had the glitter of diamonds. A big collar it was, so big that Delly had to keep a bright lookout while she was tacking around the ballroom and take care where she sat so's not to shatter it when she leaned back. But it was light and fair-fashioned as the mayflower itself, and it framed her small face the way she looked like some heaven-sent crea-

ture that was never woman of earth, still less the thing that
Delly Morgan was. It set light on her shoulders by little
glass supports under it, and they made it stand up around
her neck and close to her face, like the ruffs in old English
pictures. And somehow it caught the glints of the ballroom
in Town Hall in each leaf and flower and set them all back
on Delly's face, and wherever she walked there was that
glow on her face, strange and unaccounted, and she was
like no other woman at the Glassmakers' Ball that night.

Gaffer Morgan carried the collar to Town Hall himself,
with Slade and Delly walking on ahead. When they got
there the old man put it on her. It spread open on fine little
glass hinges and then locked in the back. No metal had a
part in it, aside from the lead the Gaffer had used in his
batch.

When Slade Morgan looked at his young wife standing
there in front of Town Hall, holding back her cape and all
rigged out in white satin underneath, with not a trinket on
her but the white mayflower collar gathering in the beams
of the street lamp and throwing the light back on her face,
the tears come to the lad's eyes. Snow was on the King's
Highway and icicles hung glittering from the eaves of
Town Hall. The mayflower collar caught the glint of the
snow, too, along with the lamplight. It made Delly look like
the cold and smiling Lady of the Frost that was in the
fairy-tale book Cap'n Freeman brought back to his chil-
dren from Copenhagen. When she smiled at Slade it was a
smile that blended with the queer tint, the silver of Sandwich glass, blended like it was something wrote down in
the formula itself.

"Don't put on your mask!" Slade cried. "You need no
mask!"

And she didn't. She went to the ball as she was, and her
face itself was a mask, and the light that was on it. Only
just before they went in, the Gaffer whispered a caution to
her.

"Don't take off the collar," he said. "Don't try to take it
off, child, without me to help you, for you might break it.
The loosing of it wants a practiced hand. I'll be home

when you come, and I'll take it off myself." And the old
man left them at the door.

He was like a man from another world, sagging along
the King's Highway back to his home, and he saw nothing,
heard nothing, with all the town laughing and singing and
making holiday around him on the streets of Sandwich, all
on their way to Town Hall. For I've mentioned what the
dances of that day was like; there wasn't nothing the match
of the Glassmakers' Ball from Plymouth to Provincetown,
year-round.

Of course Nat Maddock was there, but by the time
Slade come in with Delly and led her through the crowd,
all gaping and gasping at the sight of her, he appeared to
forget about Nat. He'd forgotten everything but Delly, and
it's my suspicion that that arbutus collar was at the bottom
of his forgetting. It's my suspicion that there was a spell in
the thing, by the way Slade Morgan acted! All he wanted
was to show Delly off to the town, to let all men see how
beautiful she was. He looked to see if they looked. And
when he saw they did, he laughed out loud. He was a man
bewitched. His eyes followed her, with a strange light in
them, while she danced the square-shuffle, and he chose to
set with the old folks during the dances and look on.

I saw other proof too, proof aplenty that there'd been
more in the making of that arbutus collar than the flesh
and bone of the hand of Shebnah Morgan. For Delly herself was acting strange and weatherwise. She kept that cold
smile like it was froze into her little white face. While the
evening was still young, she set out purposeful to ply Slade
with the drink. She had him well nigh bogged under before
long, and then, all of a sudden, she disappeared.

Nat Maddock disappeared too, and I don't know how
long the two of 'em was gone, but when Slade finally discovered it he stopped the dance.

"Delly!" he shouted through the hall, like as if he was
crying the town on fire. He tore around that ballroom like
a man shatterwitted, calling out her name, and after that
he run out and down the road.

Well, the Glassmakers' Ball wasn't a craft to founder on
the shoals of any young couple's marriage, or by the diver-

sion of any man's wife, and by and by the dancing took up
and went on as before. The fiddlers scraped away and the
seraphine struck it up, and the boding of something direful
overhanging the night was buoyed off by the music, and
with it the square-figgers began again, and the sailor's
minuet.

When it did happen, I didn't see it. Nobody saw it but
Nat Maddock. But I heard the man scream. A wild yell it
was, coming from the banks of Shawme Pond, there back
of Town Hall. That was where Nat had took Delly while
her husband was searching the streets of Sandwich for 'em.
Nat come screaming all the way back to the hall. His face
was wild and white, his hands red with blood.

He couldn't talk. He tried to tell us, but all he could do
was to point back at the Pond while the words was choking
off in his throat. Before he could lead us to Delly, several
of us was out looking through the grass on the banks of the
Pond, and in the cemetery and around the other side, near
the old Hoxie house.

Gaffer Bardo found her. He called out and all come running to him. There she lay, stretched out on the ground,
her head in a little pool that flecked slower and darker than
the pond waters. Delly Morgan's throat had been cut wide
and clean as a razor could have done.

Well, Nat Maddock was cleared on the spot when we
saw what done it—Gaffer Morgan's white arbutus collar.
The thing was mostly shattered when she fell, and the
white fragments was laying there around her head and
glinting in the moonlight where they wasn't rubied with
blood. We broke the rest of the glass away and found one
long narrow strip with an edge to it that only hard glass
can bear, imbedded in her throat.

Not everybody in Sandwich knew as much as the men at
the glasshouse did. They didn't know that Gaffer Morgan
could fashion a collar so's nobody who didn't find the hidden catch inside could get it off without sinking the virgin
edge of that blade into the throat it set around, or that the
woman who wore it couldn't be kissed without taking it off.

THE MAN WHO WAS EVERYWHERE

Edward D. Hoch

HE FIRST NOTICED THE NEW MAN IN THE NEIGHBORHOOD ON a Tuesday evening, on his way home from the station. The man was tall and thin, with a look about him that told Ray Bankcroft he was English. It wasn't anything Ray could put his finger on, the fellow just looked English.

That was all there was to their first encounter, and the second meeting passed just as casually, Friday evening at the station. The fellow was living around Pelham some place, maybe in that new apartment house in the next block.

But it was the following week that Ray began to notice him everywhere. The tall Englishman rode down to New York with Ray on the 8:09, and he was eating a few tables away at Howard Johnson's one noon. But that was the way things were in New York, Ray told himself, where you sometimes ran into the same person every day for a week, as though the laws of probability didn't exist.

It was on the weekend, when Ray and his wife journeyed up to Stamford for a picnic, that he became convinced the Englishman was following him. For there, fifty miles from home, the tall stranger came striding slowly across the rolling hills, pausing now and then to take in the beauty of the place.

"Damn it, Linda," Ray remarked to his wife, "there's that fellow again!"

"What fellow, Ray?"

"That Englishman from our neighborhood. The one I was telling you I see everywhere."

"Oh, is that him?" Linda Bankcroft frowned through the

tinted lenses of her sunglasses. "I don't remember ever seeing him before."

"Well, he must be living in that new apartment in the next block. I'd like to know what the hell he's doing up here, though. Do you think he could be following me?"

"Oh, Ray, don't be silly," Linda laughed. "Why would anyone want to follow you? And to a picnic!"

"I don't know, but it's certainly odd the way he keeps turning up. . . ."

It certainly was odd.

And as the summer passed into September, it grew odder still. Once, twice, three times a week, the mysterious Englishman appeared, always walking, always seemingly oblivious of his surroundings.

Finally, one night on Ray Bankcroft's way home, it suddenly grew to be too much for him.

He walked up to the man and asked, "Are you following me?"

The Englishman looked down his nose with a puzzled frown. "I beg your pardon?"

"Are you following me?" Ray repeated. "I see you everywhere."

"My dear chap, really, you must be mistaken."

"I'm not mistaken. Stop following me!"

But the Englishman only shook his head sadly and walked away. And Ray stood and watched him until he was out of sight. . . .

"Linda, I saw him again today!"

"Who, dear?"

"That damned Englishman! He was in the elevator in my building."

"Are you sure it was the same man?"

"Of course I'm sure! He's everywhere, I tell you! I see him every day now, on the street, on the train, at lunch, and now even in the elevator! It's driving me crazy. I'm certain he's following me. But why?"

"Have you spoken to him?"

"I've spoken to him, cursed at him, threatened him. But

it doesn't do any good. He just looks puzzled and walks away. And then the next day there he is again."

"Maybe you should call the police. But I suppose he hasn't really done anything."

"That's just the trouble, Linda. He hasn't done a single thing. It's just that he's always around. The damned thing is driving me crazy."

"What—what are you going to do about it?"

"I'll tell you what I'm going to do! The next time I see him I'm going to grab him and beat the truth out of him. I'll get to the bottom of this. . . ."

The next night, the tall Englishman was back, walking just ahead of him on the train platform. Ray ran toward him, but the Englishman disappeared in the crowd.

Perhaps the whole thing was just a coincidence, and yet . . .

Later that night Ray ran out of cigarettes, and when he left the apartment and headed for the corner drugstore, he knew the tall Englishman would be waiting for him along the route.

And as he came under the pale red glow of the flickering neon, he saw the man, walking slowly across the street from the railroad tracks.

Ray knew that this must be the final encounter.

"Say there!"

The Englishman paused and looked at him distastefully, then turned and walked away from Ray.

"Wait a minute, you! We're going to settle this once and for all!"

But the Englishman kept walking.

Ray cursed and started after him through the darkness. He called out, "Come back here!" But now the Englishman was almost running.

Ray broke into a trot, following him down the narrow street that led along the railroad tracks. "Damn you, come back! I want to talk to you!"

But the Englishman ran on, faster and faster. Finally Ray paused, out of breath.

And ahead, the Englishman had paused too.

Ray could see the gleaming glow of his wrist watch as he raised his hand in a gesture. And Ray saw that he was beckoning him to follow. . . .

Ray broke into a run again.

The Englishman waited only a moment and then he too ran, keeping close to the edge of the railroad wall, where only a few inches separated him from a twenty-foot drop to the tracks below.

In the distance, Ray heard the low whistle of the Stamford Express, tearing through the night.

Ahead, the Englishman rounded a brick wall that jutted out almost to the edge of the embankment. He was out of sight around the corner for a moment, but Ray was now almost upon him. He rounded the wall himself and saw, too late, that the Englishman was waiting for him there.

The man's big hands came at him, and all at once Ray was pushed and falling sideways, over the edge of the railroad wall, clawing helplessly at the air.

And as he hit the tracks, he saw that the Stamford Express was almost upon him, filling all space with its terrible sound. . . .

Some time later, the tall Englishman peered through a cloud of blue cigarette smoke at the graceful figure of Linda Bankcroft and said, "As I remarked at the beginning of all this, my darling, a proper murder is the ultimate game of skill. . . ."

COURTESY OF THE ROAD

Mack Morriss

CARTER BETHANE RODE STANDING UP ON THE TRUCK BED, leaning forward across the top of the cab, and the ends of his long black hair whipped against his forehead in the wind. It was like little needles sticking him, and the feel of it was constant so that gradually his forehead became numbed, and he did not notice.

Neither had he noticed the eyes of the men in the truck, the compassionate eyes, when they had stopped to pick him up and give him a ride into town. He had seen their eyes, but his mind was numb.

It had been that way for days.

When the sheriff had come, Carter Bethane was picking at the sleeve of his old G.I. shirt—the discharge shirt with the yellow emblem curled now and almost white. He had been staring at the bloodstains on the pale, much-washed cloth. The outline of the sergeant's stripes, too, had almost faded away. But the blood was fresh—a deep red— and he stared at it in the beginning of the numbness.

He had spoken slowly, in bewilderment:

"I was workin' my tobacco bed, and I seen her walkin' up toward the highway. But I didn't pay no mind. She knew to keep off the road. She was a good kid about that, she never went far. I told Ann I'd go bring her back."

He looked at the sleeve of his shirt. "I done that, all right."

The sheriff had listened uneasily. The leather of his belt and holster creaked as he shifted his weight. His question was asked almost softly: "You never seen no car, did you, Carter?"

"The hill hides the whole highway from where I was

down there. I never seen nothin', Sher'ff," Carter Bethane said, speaking slowly. "I just heard. They was just two vehicles went by."

If the sound of the word "vehicle" was strange, Carter was not aware. Any Army transport is a "vehicle," whatever its weight and size. Carter Bethane had been a soldier for a long time, longer than he had been an ex-soldier, longer than he had been home again in Tennessee, and married and a father.

"I heard 'em go down the road, wide open, one after the other. They idled off of a sudden both of 'em, when they was right along here. Then they opened up again. I never paid no mind, then."

The sheriff's leather creaked more loudly. "Well, I'm sorry, son. You can't identify no speedin' car by ear—not with you on the other side of a hill. Any lawyer'd tear you apart on the stand."

The young man had stood silently, pulling at his sleeve, and there was silence on the stretch of the road. "Yeah," he said. "I guess a lawyer would."

"We'll do all we can, son. . . ."

"I'll be much obliged to you Sher'ff. She's dead now. They ain't much any of us can do."

"Not unless we just happen to be lucky, son."

"I guess that's right. I ain't never been what you call real lucky. Have you, Sher'ff?"

"I'm sorry, son," the sheriff said. "We'll do all we can, anyway. It's hard, without no witnesses. It'd just have to be almost an accident, you might say, if we ever get justice in a case like this here. I doubt she even made a dent, she was such a little thing—"

He no longer heard the sheriff, for the numbness was complete. The sheriff turned away and spoke roughly to his deputies. "Let's go on up to Gillys'," he said. "They was a call about some more trouble up there again. It looks like some people was just born mean." He turned again to Carter and said, "I'm sorry, son. We'll do what we can." The young man did not feel the sheriff touch him, awkwardly.

Carter Bethane stood now, swaying easily on wide-braced legs, and watched as the narrow black-top highway slid itself under the truck, twisting and heaving and falling away in the manner of mountain roads. From the cab below him there was a shouted phrase of conversation, sounding far away and weak beneath the sounds of the truck's vibration and of wind in his ears.

A horn sounded inquisitively behind him, and Carter Bethane moved his arm absently in a motion that indicated the road ahead was clear. It was a courtesy of the road, practiced throughout the mountains. The car moved ahead with assurance. The young man glanced at it, and his benumbed mind made record: '36 Chivalay sedan.

The young man was of a generation that had trained itself to know automobile makes and models as a matter of young pride, and the training had been useful in wartime, for it had become integrated into the life of the generation. A car had become a mechanical extension of life in the mountains, as once the rifle had been; and like the rifle it was an implement of death.

Leaning on the cab of the truck, rolling with the tilt of the wide truck bed, Carter Bethane stood numb in the cooling wind. He watched blankly as the truck lay, now left, now right, into the familiar curves of the road to town. There was no need to concentrate upon the road: Carter Bethane knew it intimately, and its curving route was like a friend to him in his helpless anger and pain.

He did not turn until he heard again the sound of a horn.

The jeep was bright orange, with GILLY BROTHERS SERVICE STATION lettered on its windshield frame. Its driver stared at the young man on the truck bed, then peered around the truck to see the curving road ahead. Carter faced the wind; without turning again he signaled the driver to wait, to remain in line. A car coming toward them zipped by.

The jeep moved impatiently left, toward the center of the road. Carter's hand waved him back. Again a car went by in the opposite lane.

The truck, with the jeep close under its tail gate, went into a long S curve: right, then left, then right again, downhill at first, then up on the middle curve. The jeep popped flatly its old familiar exhaust, an unforgettable, unmistakable sound as its engine idled in the coasting down. The driver watched Carter's hand.

The numbness of Carter Bethane's forehead was deeper now, the wind stronger as he faced it. But his mind in an instant had become sharp and clear. At the other end of the S, on the opposite hill, he saw a flash of orange. He watched it, coldly calculating, and no longer helpless. He looked back at the orange jeep behind. The driver's eyes were fixed on Carter; they lifted slightly from the warning hand. For a moment the two men stared at each other as if hypnotized by the sensation of air and speed.

Then as he felt the truck lean left into the body of the S, Carter Bethane shifted to keep his balance, faced the wind once more and braced himself. He felt the truck bed press upward against his feet, starting the uphill swing, at the bend of the middle curve. He changed his signal and waved the jeep ahead with a long graceful movement of his left arm then—a movement of certainty, of absolute assurance.

The impatient jeep behind shot instantly to the left as its accelerator was kicked viciously. The crash of orange against orange at the curve was much louder than the rush of the wind.

The truck braked to a stop, and Carter Bethane and the three men in the cab jumped out and ran back toward the smashed-up jeeps. There was silence, complete and soothing after the wind. The men's voices sounded muffled in it. At first they shouted, but then they spoke softly, from habit, and with awe.

"Both the Gilly boys—head on."

"Lord, look at 'em! They never would let nobody else drive them jeeps. If you didn't know that, you wouldn't hardly know who it was, would you?"

They shuffled their feet, watching a wheel spin slower and slower. "I knowed somethin'd happen to 'em one of these days, the way the crazy fools drove."

When the wheel stopped, the man who had spoken last said, "Well, let's go call the sher'ff. They ain't nothin' we can do here." Then he said, "I reckon this'll be the last trouble the sher'ff goin' to have with the Gilly boys. Lord knows he had enough, him and a lot of other people. It looked like them two was just born mean, sneakin' mean."

He turned to Carter and, in the irrelevant way of men shocked, he asked, "Ridin' all right back there, son? I'd forgot about you."

Carter nodded, then added in the same soft tone, "I was goin' to ride up to the station with one of 'em, instead of goin' into town. I heard one of the jeeps go down 'while ago, an' I figured he'd be comin' back about now."

"You'd have waited on him a mighty long time."

"No," Carter said, climbing over the tail gate. "I didn't figure on waitin' too long, one way or another, on either one of 'em."

The men on the ground didn't hear. Still in awe, one of them said, "It's funny, ain't it, when you think about it? Them was just about the only two jeeps you ever saw on this road."

The men climbed in, and the truck was on its way. Leaning across the top of the cab once more, Carter Bethane reflected that the trip to town was useless for him now. He might not have needed more than the two rounds of ammunition that were in the .45 automatic inside his shirt. But it would have been better to have had the magazine full. It didn't matter now.

A horn sounded behind him again, and Carter Bethane's hand moved instantly to a signal of caution. They were approaching another curve in the road.

REMAINS TO BE SEEN

Jack Ritchie

"I AM A CITIZEN AND A TAXPAYER," I SAID STIFFLY. "WHEN you are through with this destructive invasion of my property, I demand that everything be restored to its exact and original condition."

"Now don't you worry about that, Mr. Warren," Detective-sergeant Littler said. "The city will put everything in apple-pie order again." He smiled. "Whether we find anything or not."

He was, of course, referring to the body of my wife.

So far they hadn't found it.

"You're going to have quite a job of repair, Sergeant. Your men have practically excavated the garden. The front lawn resembles a plowed field. You are apparently dismantling my house, piece by piece, and now I see that your men are carrying a jackhammer into the basement."

We were in the kitchen and Littler sipped coffee.

He still bathed in confidence. "The total area of the United States is 3,026,789 square miles, including water."

Littler had undoubtedly memorized the figure for just such occasions.

"Does that include the Hawaiian Islands and Alaska?" I asked acidly.

He was not ruffled. "I think we can exclude them. As I said, the total area of the United States is 3,026,789 square miles. This encompasses mountains and plains, cities and farmland, desert and water. And yet when a man kills his wife, he invariably buries her within the confines of his own property."

Certainly the safest place, I thought. If one buried one's wife in the woods, invariably some trespassing Boy Scout digging for arrowheads would uncover her.

Littler smiled again. "Just how big is your lot?"

"Sixty by one hundred and fifty feet. Do you realize that I worked for years to produce the loam in my garden? Your men have burrowed into the subsoil and now I see yellow streaks of clay all about."

He had been here two hours and he was still certain of success. "I'm afraid that you'll have more than the tilth of your garden to worry about, Mr. Warren."

The kitchen window gave me a view of the backyard. Eight or ten city laborers, supervised by the police, were turning the area into a series of trenches.

Littler watched them. "We are very thorough. We will analyze the soot of your chimney; we will sift the ashes from your furnace."

"I have oil heating." I poured more coffee. "I did not kill my wife. I do not, in fact, know where she is."

Littler helped himself to sugar. "How do you account for her absence?"

"I do not account for her absence. Emily simply packed a suitcase during the night and left me. You did notice that some of her clothing is missing?"

"How do I know what she had?" Littler glanced at the photograph of my wife I had provided for him. "Meaning no offense, why did you marry her?"

"For love, of course."

But that was patently ridiculous and even the sergeant didn't believe it.

"Your wife was insured for ten thousand dollars, wasn't she? And you are the beneficiary?"

"Yes." The insurance had certainly been a factor for her demise, but it had not been my primary motive. I got rid of Emily for the honest reason that I couldn't stand her any more.

I will not say that, when I married Emily, I was in the throes of flaming passion. My constitution is not shaped in that manner. I believe I entered into matrimony principally because I succumbed to the common herd-feeling of guilt at prolonged bachelorhood.

Emily and I had both been employed by the Marshall Paper Products Company—I as a senior accountant and Emily as a plodding typist without any prospect of matrimony in her future.

She was plain, quiet, subdued. She did not know how to dress properly, her conversation never soared beyond observations on the weather, and she exercised her intellect by reading the newspaper on alternate days.

In short, she was the ideal wife for a man who feels that marriage should be an arrangement, not a romance.

But it is utterly amazing how, once the security of marriage is established, a plain, quiet, subdued woman can turn into a determined shrew.

The woman should at least have been grateful.

"How did you and your wife get along?"

Miserably. But I said, "We had our differences, but then doesn't everyone?"

The sergeant, however, was equipped with superior information. "According to your neighbors, you and your wife quarreled almost incessantly."

By neighbors, he was undoubtedly referring to Fred and Wilma Treeber. Since I have a corner lot, theirs is the only house directly next door. I doubt if Emily's voice carried over the garden and the alley to the Morrisons. Still, it was possible. As she gained weight, she gained volume.

"The Treebers could hear you and your wife arguing nearly every evening."

"Only when they stopped their own infernal shrieking to listen. And it is not true that they heard *both* of us. I never raise my voice."

"The last time your wife was seen alive was Friday evening at six-thirty as she entered this house."

Yes, she had returned from the supermarket with frozen dinners and ice cream. They were almost her sole contribution to the art of cooking. I made my own breakfasts, I ate lunch at the company cafeteria, and in the evening I either made my own meal or ate something that required forty minutes of heating at 350°.

"That was the last time anyone *else* saw her," I said. "But I last saw her in the evening when we retired. And in the morning when I woke, I discovered that she had packed up and gone."

Downstairs, the jackhammer began breaking up the concrete floor. It made so much noise that I was forced to close the door to the rear entry leading to the basement. "Just who was it who saw Emily last? Besides myself, I mean."

"Mr. and Mrs. Fred Treeber."

There was a certain resemblance between Wilma Treeber and Emily. They had both become large women, Amazon in temper and dwarf in mind. Fred Treeber is a small man, watery-eyed by nature or by the abrasions of marriage. But he plays a credible game of chess and he rather admires me for possessing the inherent firmness that he lacks.

"At midnight that same evening," Sergeant Littler said, "Fred Treeber heard an unearthly scream coming from this house."

"Unearthly?"

"His exact word."

"Fred Treeber is a liar," I said flatly. "I suppose his wife heard it, too?"

"No. She's a heavy sleeper. But it woke him."

"Did this so-called unearthly scream wake up the Morrisons?"

"No. They were asleep, too, and they are also a considerable distance from this house. The Treeber place is only fifteen feet away." Littler filled his pipe. "Fred Treeber debated waking his wife, but decided against it. It seems she has a temper. But still he couldn't go back to sleep. And then at two in the morning, he heard a noise coming from your yard. He went to the window and there, in the moonlight, he saw you digging in your garden. He finally got up the nerve to wake his wife. They both watched you."

"The wretched spies. So that was how you knew?"

"Yes. Why did you use such a large box?"

"It was the only one I could find. But it was still not anywhere near the dimensions of a coffin."

"Mrs. Treeber thought about that all day Saturday. And when you informed her that your wife had 'taken a trip and wouldn't be back for some time,' she finally decided that you had . . . ah . . . organized your wife's body into a more compact package and buried her."

I poured more coffee for myself. "Well, and what did you find?"

He was still faintly embarrassed about that. "A dead cat."

I nodded. "And so I am guilty of burying a cat."

He smiled. "You were very evasive, Mr. Warren. First you denied that you had buried anything."

"I felt that it was none of your business."

"And when we found the cat, you claimed that it had died of natural causes."

"So it appeared to me at the time."

"The cat was your wife's and someone had crushed its skull. That was obvious."

"I am not in the habit of examining dead cats."

He puffed at his pipe. "It's my theory that after you killed your wife, you also killed the cat. Perhaps because its presence reminded you of your wife. Or perhaps because the cat had seen you dispose of your wife's body and just might lead us . . ."

"Oh, come now, Sergeant," I said.

He colored. "Well, animals *have* been known to dig at places where their masters or mistresses have been buried. Dogs, usually, I'll admit. But why not cats?"

I actually gave that some thought. Why not cats?

Littler listened to the jackhammer for a moment. "When we get a report that someone is missing, our routine procedure is to send out flyers through the Missing Persons' Bureau. And then we wait. Almost invariably after a week or two the missing person returns home. Usually, after his money runs out."

"And then why in heaven's name didn't you do that in this case? I'm sure that Emily will come back home within a few days. As far as I know she took only about a hundred dollars and I know that she is mortally frightened of self-support."

His teeth showed faintly. "When we have a missing wife, a person who hears a scream, and two witnesses to a mysterious moonlight burial in a garden, we recognize all the symptoms of a crime. We cannot affort to wait."

And neither could I. After all, Emily's body would not keep forever. That was why I had killed the cat and managed to be seen burying the box. But I spoke acidly. "And so you immediately grab your shovels and ruin a man's property? I warn you that I will sue if every stick, stone, brick, and scrap of humus isn't replaced exactly as it was."

Littler was unperturbed. "And then there was the blood stain on your living room rug."

"My own blood, I assure you. I accidently broke a glass and gashed my hand." I showed him the healing cut again.

He was not impressed. "A cover-up to account for the stain," he said. "Self-inflicted."

He was right, of course. But I wanted the spot on the rug in the event that the other circumstances were not enough to drive the police to their search.

I saw Fred Treeber leaning on the boundary fence watching Littler's men at their devastation.

I got to my feet. "I'm going to talk to that creature."

Littler followed me outside.

I made my way between mounds of earth to the fence. "Do you call this being a good neighbor?"

Fred Treeber swallowed. "Now, Albert, I didn't mean any harm. I don't think you really did it, but you know Wilma and her imagination."

I glared at him. "There will be no more chess games between us in the future." I turned to Littler. "What makes you so absolutely positive that I disposed of my wife here?"

Littler took the pipe out of his mouth. "Your car. You took it to the Engle Filling Station on Murray Street Friday afternoon at five-thirty. You had the car lubricated and the oil changed. The attendant placed the usual sticker inside the doorframe of your car, indicating when the work was done and the mileage on your speedometer at the time it was done. Since that time, the only additional mileage registered by your car has been eight-tenths of a mile. And that is the exact distance from the filling station to your garage."

He smiled. "In other words, you brought your car directly home. You do not work on Saturdays and today is Sunday. Your car hasn't moved since Friday."

I had been counting on the police to notice that sticker. If they hadn't, I would have had to call it to their attention in some manner. I smiled thinly. "Have you ever thought of the possibility that I might have carried her to an empty lot near here and buried her?"

Littler chuckled indulgently. "The nearest empty lot is more than four blocks away. It hardly seems conceivable that you would carry her body through the streets, even at night, for that distance."

Treeber took his eyes from the group of men at my flower patch. "Albert, as long as your dahlias are being dug up anyway, would you care to trade a few of your Gordon Pinks for some of my Amber Goliaths?"

I turned on my heel and stalked back to the house.

The afternoon wore on, and gradually, as he received reports from his men, the assurance drained from Littler's face.

The daylight faded, and at six-thirty the jackhammer in the basement stopped.

A Sergeant Chilton came into the kitchen. He looked tired, hungry, and frustrated, and his trousers were streaked with clay. "Nothing down there. Absolutely nothing at all."

Littler clamped his teeth on his pipe stem. "You're positive? You've searched everywhere?"

"I'll stake my life on it," Chilton said. "If there's a body anywhere here, we would have found it. The men outside are through, too."

Littler glared at me. "I *know* you killed your wife. I *feel* it."

There is something pitiful about a normally intelligent man retreating to instinct. However, in this case, he was right.

"I believe I'll make myself liver and onions tonight," I said cheerfully. "I haven't had that for ages."

A patrolman came into the kitchen from the backyard. "Sergeant, I was just talking to this Treeber character next door."

"Well?" Littler demanded impatiently.

"He says that Mr. Warren here has a summer cottage at a lake in Byron County."

I almost dropped the package of liver I was removing from the refrigerator. That idiot Treeber and his babbling!

Littler's eyes widened. His humor changed instantly and he chuckled. "That's it! They *always, always* bury them on their own property."

Perhaps my face was white. "Don't you dare touch one foot of that land. I put two thousand dollars' worth of improvement on that property since I bought it and I will not have the place blitzed by your vandals."

Littler laughed. "Chilton, get some floodlights and have the men pack up." He turned to me. "And now just where is this little retreat of yours?"

"I absolutely refuse to tell you. You know I couldn't have gone there anyway. You forget that the speedometer reading of my car shows that it hasn't left the garage since Friday afternoon."

He hurdled that obstacle. "You could have set the speedometer back. Now where is that cottage located?"

I folded my arms. "I refuse to tell you."

Littler smiled. "There's no use stalling for time. Or do you plan to sneak out there yourself tonight, disinter her, and bury her someplace else?"

"I have no intentions of the kind. But I stand on my constitutional rights to say nothing."

Littler used my phone to route out officials in Byron county and within forty-five minutes, he had the exact location of my cottage.

"Now see here," I snapped as he put down the phone for the last time. "You can't make the same mess out of that place as you have of this one. I'm going to call the mayor right now and see that you're fired."

Littler was in a good humor and practically rubbing his hands. "Chilton, see that a crew gets here tomorrow and puts everything back in place."

I followed Littler to the door. "Every flower, every blade of grass, or I'll see my lawyer."

I did not enjoy my liver and onions that night.

At eleven-thirty, there was a soft knock at my rear door and I opened it.

Fred Treeber looked contrite. "I'm sorry."

"What in heaven's name made you mention the cottage?"

"I was just making conversation and it slipped out."

I had difficulty controlling my rage. "They'll devastate the place. And just after I finally succeeded in producing a good lawn."

I could have gone on for more furious minutes, but I pulled myself together. "Is your wife asleep?"

Fred nodded. "She won't wake up until morning. She never does."

I got my hat and coat and we went next door to Fred's basement.

Emily's body was lying in a cool place under some canvas. I thought it had been a rather good temporary hiding place. Wilma never goes down there except on washdays.

Fred and I carried Emily back to my house and into the basement. The place looked like a battlefield.

We dropped Emily into one of the deepest pits and shoveled about a foot and a half of clay and dirt over her. That was sufficient for our purposes.

Fred looked a bit worried. "Are you sure they won't find her?"

"Of course not. The best place to hide anything is where somebody has already looked. Tomorrow the crew will be back here. The holes will be filled up and the floor refinished."

We went upstairs into the kitchen.

"Do I have to wait a whole year?" Fred asked me plaintively.

"Certainly. We can't flirt with suspicion. After twelve months or so, you may murder your wife and I will keep her in *my* basement until the search of your premises is over."

Fred sighed. "It's a long time to wait with Wilma. But we flipped the coin, fair and square, and you won." He cleared his throat. "You didn't really mean that, did you, Albert?"

"Mean what?"

"That you'd never play chess with me again?"

When I thought about what the police were at this very moment undoubtedly doing to my cottage and its grounds, I was tempted to tell him I had meant it.

But he did look pathetic and contrite, and so I sighed and said, "I suppose not."

Fred brightened. "I'll go get the board."

THE MAN WHO SOLD
ROPE TO THE GNOLES

Idris Seabright

THE GNOLES HAD A BAD REPUTATION, AND MORTENSEN WAS quite aware of this. But he reasoned, correctly enough, that cordage must be something for which the gnoles had a long unsatisfied want, and he saw no reason why he should not be the one to sell it to them. What a triumph such a sale would be! The district sales manager might single out Mortensen for special mention at the annual sales-force dinner. It would help his sales quota enormously. And, after all, it was none of his business what the gnoles used cordage for.

Mortensen decided to call on the gnoles on Thursday morning. On Wednesday night he went through his *Manual of Modern Salesmanship*, underscoring things.

"The mental states through which the mind passes in making a purchase," he read, "have been catalogued as: 1) arousal of interest; 2) increase of knowledge; 3) adjustment to needs . . ." There were seven mental states listed, and Mortensen underscored all of them. Then he went back and double-scored No. 1, arousal of interest, No. 4, appreciation of suitability, and No. 7, decision to purchase. He turned the page.

"Two qualities are of exceptional importance to a salesman," he read. "They are adaptability and knowledge of merchandise." Mortensen underlined the qualities. "Other highly desirable attributes are physical fitness, and high ethical standard, charm of manner, a dogged persistence, and unfailing courtesy." Mortensen underlined these, too. But he read on to the end of the paragraph without underscoring anything more, and it may be that his failure to put "tact and keen power of observation" on a footing with the other attributes of a salesman was responsible for what happened to him.

The gnoles live on the very edge of Terra Cognita, on the far side of a wood which all authorities unite in describing as dubious. Their house is narrow and high, in architecture a blend of Victorian Gothic and Swiss chalet. Though the house needs paint, it is kept in good repair. Thither on Thursday morning, sample case in hand, Mortensen took his way.

No path leads to the house of the gnoles, and it is always dark in that dubious wood. But Mortensen, remembering what he had learned at his mother's knee concerning the odor of gnoles, found the house quite easily. For a moment he stood hesitating before it. His lips moved as he repeated, "Good morning, I have come to supply your cordage requirements," to himself. The words were the beginning of his sales talk. Then he went up and rapped on the door.

The gnoles were watching him through holes that had bored in the trunks of trees; it is an artful custom of theirs to which the prime authority on gnoles attests. Mortensen's knock almost threw them into confusion, it was so long since anyone had knocked at their door. Then the senior gnole, the one who never leaves the house, went flitting up from the cellars and opened it.

The senior gnole is a little like a Jerusalem artichoke made of India rubber, and he has small red eyes which are faceted in the same way that gemstones are. Mortensen had been expecting something unusual, and when the gnole opened the door he bowed politely, took off his hat, and smiled. He had got past the sentence about cordage requirements and into an enumeration of the different types of cordage his firm manufactured when the gnole, by turning his head to the side, showed him that he had no ears. Nor was there anything on his head which could take their place in the conduction of sound. Then the gnole opened his little fanged mouth and let Mortensen look at his narrow, ribbony tongue. As a tongue it was no more fit for human speech than was a serpent's. Judging from his appearance, the gnole could not safely be assigned to any of the four physio-characterological types mentioned in the

Manual; and for the first time Mortensen felt a definite qualm.

Nonetheless, he followed the gnole unhesitatingly when the creature motioned him within. Adaptability, he told himself, adaptability must be his watchword. Enough adaptability, and his knees might even lose their tendency to shakiness.

It was the parlor the gnole led him to. Mortensen's eyes widened as he looked around it. There were whatnots in the corners, and cabinets of curiosities, and on the fretwork table an album with gilded hasps; who knows whose pictures were in it? All around the walls in brackets, where in lesser houses the people display ornamental plates, were emeralds as big as your head. The gnoles set great store by their emeralds. All the light in the dim room came from them.

Mortensen went through the phrases of his sales talk mentally. It distressed him that that was the only way he could go through them. Still, adaptability! The gnole's interest was already aroused, or he would never have asked Mortensen into the parlor; and as soon as the gnole saw the various cordages the sample case contained, he would no doubt proceed of his own accord through "appreciation of suitability" to "desire to process."

Mortensen sat down in the chair the gnole indicated and opened his sample case. He got out henequen cable-laid rope, an assortment of ply and yarn goods, and some superlative slender abaca fiber rope. He even showed the gnole a few soft yarns and twines made of cotton and jute.

On the back of an envelope he wrote prices for hanks and cheeses of the twines, and for fifty- and hundred-foot lengths of the ropes. Laboriously he added details about the strength, durability, and resistance to climatic conditions of each sort of cord. The senior gnole watched him intently, putting his little feet on the top rung of his chair and poking at the facets of his left eye now and then with a tentacle. In the cellars from time to time someone would scream.

Mortensen began to demonstrate his wares. He showed the gnole the slip and resilience of one rope, the tenacity and stubborn strength of another. He cut a tarred hemp rope in two and laid a five-foot piece on the parlor floor to show the gnole how absolutely "neutral" it was, with no tendency to untwist of its own accord. He even showed the gnole how nicely some of the cotton twines made up in square knotwork.

They settled at last on two ropes of abaca fiber, 3/16 and 5/8 inch in diameter. The gnole wanted an enormous quantity. Mortensen's comment on those ropes, "unlimited strength and durability," seemed to have attracted him.

Soberly Mortensen wrote the particulars down in his order book, but ambition was setting his brain on fire. The gnoles, it seemed, would be regular customers; and after the gnoles, why should he not try the Gibbelins? They too must have a need for rope.

Mortensen closed his order book. On the back of the same envelope he wrote, for the gnole to see, that delivery would be made within ten days. Terms were 30 percent with order, balance upon receipt of goods.

The senior gnole hesitated. Shyly he looked at Mortensen with his little red eyes. Then he got down the smallest of the emeralds from the wall and handed it to him.

The sales representative stood weighing it in his hands. It was the smallest of the gnoles' emeralds, but it was as clear as water, as green as grass. In the outside world it would have ransomed a Rockefeller or a whole family of Guggenheims; a legitimate profit from a transaction was one thing, but this was another; "a high ethical standard" —any kind of ethical standard—would forbid Mortensen to keep it. He weighed it a moment longer. Then with a deep, deep sigh he gave the emerald back.

He cast a glance around the room to see if he could find something which would be more negotiable. And in an evil moment he fixed on the senior gnole's auxiliary eyes.

The senior gnole keeps his extra pair of optics on the third shelf of the curiosity cabinet with the glass doors. They look like fine dark emeralds about the size of the end of your thumb. And if the gnoles in general set store by their gems, it is nothing at all compared to the senior gnole's emotions about his extra eyes. The concern good

Christian folk should feel for their soul's welfare is a shadow, a figment, a nothing, compared to what the thoroughly heathen gnole feels for those eyes. He would rather, I think, choose to be a mere miserable human being than that some vandal should lay hands upon them.

If Mortensen had not been elated by his success to the point of anaesthesia, he would have seen the gnole stiffen, he would have heard him hiss, when he went over to the cabinet. All innocent, Mortensen opened the glass door, took the twin eyes out, and juggled them sacrilegiously in his hand; the gnole could feel them clink. Smiling to evince the charm of manner advised in the *Manual*, and raising his brows as one who says, "Thank you, these will do nicely," Mortensen dropped the eyes into his pocket.

The gnole growled.

The growl awoke Mortensen from his trance of euphoria. It was a growl whose meaning no one could mistake. This was clearly no time to be doggedly persistent. Mortensen made a break for the door.

The senior gnole was there before him, his network of tentacles outstretched. He caught Mortensen in them easily and wound them, flat as bandages, around his ankles and his hands. The best abaca fiber is no stronger then those tentacles; though the gnoles would find rope a convenience, they get along very well without it. Would you, dear reader, go naked if zippers should cease to be made? Growling indignantly, the gnole fished his ravished eyes from Mortensen's pockets, and then carried him down to the cellar to the fattening pens.

But great are the virtues of legitimate commerce. Though they fattened Mortensen sedulously, and, later, roasted and sauced him and ate him with real appetite, the gnoles slaughtered him in quite a humane manner and never once thought of torturing him. That is unusual, for gnoles. And they ornamented the plank on which they served him with a beautiful border of fancy knotwork made of cotton cord from his own sample case.

LOST DOG

Henry Slesar

THE COUCH IN DR. FROHLICH'S WAITING ROOM WAS
severely modern, covered with a stylish but nubby fabric
that rubbed unpleasantly against the silken fabric of Julia
Smollett's dress. She sighed and leaned forward, folding her
small white hands in her lap, hugging her thin arms against
her side. She looked young and vulnerable and sweetly
pathetic, and the man she had married fourteen years ago
looked at her and frowned.

George was standing on the other side of the room, examining a hunting print. He was thick in the chest and
short in the arms, and he wore subdued tweeds. There was
a round collar on his short neck, clasped by a small gold
pin. His trousers were narrow, and his jacket closely fitted.
He looked like a man accustomed to riding habits, thick
leather straps, saddle soap, and early morning walks.
Actually, he was a city-bred accountant, with an office on
Lexington Avenue.

Julia sighed again, conversationally.

"Well, what is it?" her husband asked.

"Nothing. I just feel—tired. Why is he taking so long?"

"We've only been here five minutes. God, what a time-
sense women have!"

She turned mournful eyes at him, large damp eyes of
deep violet, to which he had once written a sixteen-line
verse. "I'm sorry," she said quietly. "It just seems long."

Then a knowing, redheaded woman came into the room,
looked them over critically, and said, "Mr. and Mrs.
Smollett? Dr. Frohlich's ready now."

The doctor was behind the desk of a pleasant, woody

office. He was a plump, amiable man, with soft gray, close-cropped hair.

"Very glad you came, Mr. Smollett," he said. "I told your wife that I thought it would be helpful if you were here when we performed our little experiment. I thought, perhaps, you could supply a little more background. . . ."

George Smollett cleared his throat. "Now look, Dr. Frohlich." He spoke in candid tones. "I don't want you to get the wrong idea. I'm not one of these superstitious people who think hypnotism is some kind of black magic. I mean, I've read things. I know."

"Good," the doctor nodded. "The attitude will help. It's getting past that first prejudice that counts. Your wife, of course, is pretty well used to the idea by now. Eh, Mrs. Smollett?"

Even in the small office chair, Julia looked tiny. She smiled hesitatingly, and nodded.

"We've had many rewarding chats, your wife and I. We understand each other. We have an appreciation of what our problems will be. But I thought, before we actually attempt our age-regression experiment, that your own views should be expressed."

"Well." George Smollett rubbed his jaw. "I'm not sure I understand you."

"Nothing very involved. I'd just like to know how you feel about your wife's fear of dogs. As I understand things, it was your suggestion that she get medical help."

"Oh. Yes, that was my idea. You see, my wife's a very timid woman, Dr. Frohlich. I don't have to tell you. I mean, it wasn't so bad when we were first married. I think it might have started after George, Junior, was born. Our first child; he's eleven now. Then it got really bad. I mean, there wasn't anything that didn't frighten her. Noises. Darkness. Anything! And as for dogs—" He made an expressive gesture with his shoulder.

"Yes," the doctor said. "Tell me about the dogs."

The husband studied the unusual lamp on the desk. "Don't ask me to explain. That's your department. All I know is that she's so scared of dogs that if she sees one— just sees one, understand, a mile off—she gets hysterical.

Now this has been going on for a long time. Only now it's worse."

"In what way is it worse?"

"Well, because we moved this year. To the country. Up to Wister County. I mean, you know how these communities are, Doctor. There's a million dogs around. Everybody's got a pooch."

A strained sound came from Julia's direction. Both doctor and husband chose to ignore it.

"Did you know this when you moved?"

George didn't like the question. "I never gave it much thought. I guess I forgot about this phobia of hers. But if you ask me, the best way to cure somebody of a thing like this is to make them face up to it—"

"I agree with you," the doctor said. "With certain reservations."

"There!" Her husband's triumphant look swept the woman like a beacon. "What'd I tell you, Julia?" He turned to Frohlich again, and smiled. "My idea was to get a dog ourselves. A good, man-sized dog, like a Dane. I mean, we have two boys, Dr. Frohlich. You know what boys are like. When I was a kid, I always had a dog. It's a shame to deprive the kid, isn't it?"

"They can be good companions," the doctor said guardedly.

"Sure they can! Listen, you just can't beat a dog for loyalty. And in a place like that—I mean, out in the country and all, with tramps and so forth around—well, a dog's a necessity in a place like that. Don't you think so?"

"Perhaps."

"Sure. Well, that was my first idea. Just bring home a dog and let her get used to it. I had my eye on this Great Dane I saw at a kennel up around Hawthorne Lake. A real man-sized animal, no lap dog, you know what I mean? A dog that can take care of itself. . . ."

Julia shuddered.

"But I didn't get him," the husband sighed. "I just couldn't take the commotion. That's about the only time you hear a peep out of Julia—when you cross her. So I suggested that maybe she get medical attention. That's when we saw Dr. Ellison. And he recommended we see you. So——" He spread his palms.

"Fine," Dr. Frohlich said. "Now I think I owe you a few words. About what I plan to do today." He leaned back in his chair.

"I've already told Mrs. Smollett quite a lot about hypnotic techniques in psychoanalysis. I won't bore her by repeating it all. But briefly, for your sake, I want to say this. In psychoanalysis, we consider hypnotism a valuable form of therapy. We find it useful in many special instances. It can often save the patient many, many months, because it so quickly eliminates his—natural resistance. You know what transference is?"

"I think so."

"Yes. Well, hypnosis provides a sort of immediate transference between doctor and patient. It brings us both closer to the source of the problem. And in a case like your wife's where I believe her fear of dogs is rooted in a past incident long repressed, it may be very helpful in lifting, you might say, the curtain which has dropped over her subconscious."

"I see," George said. He looked sideways at his wife. Julia was watching the doctor's moving lips.

"It is not always a miraculous cure, however," Frohlich warned. "I must make that clear. It is usually no substitute for thorough analysis. It's only a tool." He must have seen Julia's mouth droop, because he smiled and added:

"But I feel rather optimistic about Mrs. Smollett's recovery. I honestly do. By applying age-regression techniques, I think we can accomplish a great deal. And that is what I plan to do today."

"Just what does that mean, Doctor? Age-regression?"

Frohlich stood up. "I'm going to take your wife back into her own past. I'm going to ask her to relive her early years, and see if we can't peek under that curtain. . . ."

"Now?" Julia said softly.

"If you are ready. Yes, now." He pushed the white button set in the side of his desk, and the knowing redhead appeared. She began to draw the blinds, covering up the gray sky and misty rain on view from the window.

"If you'll be so good," the doctor said, "as to wait outside for a while, Mr. Smollett—"

"Yes, of course."

"I'll ask you to return when your wife is in the trance state. I think you might find what follows very enlightening."

"Yes," George said uncertainly. Then he went to the door.

It was dark in the room now, and Dr. Frohlich switched on the odd-shaped desk lamp. It shown in Julia Smollett's face as the doctor approached her.

The redhead said: "All right, Mr. Smollett."

The room was still dark when George reentered. Frohlich was sitting on the edge of his desk, toying with a metal fountain pen. Julia was in the same chair, her shoulders slumped, her hands locked limply in her lap. The large eyes were closed.

"Is she—"

"Oh, yes," the doctor said. "Your wife is quite suggestible. It doesn't take us more than five or ten minutes. Now I'll ask you to sit quietly on that side of the room, while I conduct my questioning."

George took a seat in the corner, near a crowded bookcase. The doctor leaned towards his wife.

"You may open your eyes now, Julia."

She did. They seemed disinterested, but not staring. George swallowed hard.

"Do you know what day it is today, Julia?"

"Yes. Wednesday."

"No, you are wrong. It is Friday, Julia. Is that right?"

"Yes. Friday."

"No, Julia. It is not Friday, either. Do you know what day it is now?"

She hesitated, her lips moving. "No. I don't know what day it is."

The doctor looked toward her husband. "I am purposely doing this. I wish to dislocate her in Time." He continued the questioning, until the woman admitted to no knowledge of the month and year.

"Julia, listen to me. I'm going to ask you to go back to your past. You are going to be a child all over again. You are going to relive your life from the time you were a little girl. You are going to see and hear and feel everything you did since you were a baby. And you are going to tell me everything I want to know about what you see, hear, and feel. You are going to answer all my questions, starting right now. . . ."

He leaned closer, and a subtle change was coming over the woman's small, tight features.

"You are one year old now, Julia. You are an infant only one year old. Tell me what I want to know, Julia. Tell me if you are afraid of dogs?"

When George Smollett heard the answer that came from his wife's lips, he started. It was in a voice so tiny and indistinct, so eerie and unnatural, that even Dr. Frohlich reacted with some surprise.

"No," the strange voice told them. "No, I'm not afraid of dogs. . . ."

"Now you are two," the doctor said. "You are two years old, Julia. Are you afraid of dogs?"

"No," the voice said again, and her pinched face was screwed into an odd contortion. "I'm not afraid of bow-wow. I'm not afraid . . ."

"You are three years old, Julia. You are three years old. Tell me. Are you afraid of dogs?"

The voice was stronger. "No. I'm not afraid."

"You are four, Julia. You are four years old."

The years of her childhood flashed by in her voice and in her face. Then the doctor was saying:

"You are ten years old, Julia. Now you are ten. Are you afraid of dogs? Are you afraid of dogs, Julia?"

It was the moment Frohlich was seeking. The contorted face was changing again, and the woman's thin body was squirming in the chair. Then her white hands were balling into fists, and the fists were rubbing at the large eyes. Tears came, and she sobbed.

"Topper," she said, gulping. "Topper . . ."

Eagerly, Frohlich said: "Who is Topper, Julia?"

"Topper," the girl cried. "Poor Topper!"

"Who is Topper, Julia? Is Topper a dog?"

"Yes." She nodded. "Yes. Topper is my dog. Topper is a good dog."

"Where is Topper now, Julia?"

"Topper is dead!" she wailed. "They put Topper away! They killed him! And it's my fault! It's my fault!"

The sobs ended abruptly, and the young voice hardened. "It's his fault. It's Bobby's fault."

"Who is Bobby, Julia?"

"I hate him!" Her fist struck her knee. "I hate him! He's mean! Bobby's mean!"

"Who is he, Julia? Is Bobby a friend of yours?"

"I hate him! He teases me! He teases me all the time. I'm glad I did it. I'm glad! Only don't kill Topper. Please don't kill Topper!"

Frohlich wiped the moisture from his forehead.

"I want you to tell me all about it, Julia. I want you to tell me about Bobby, and Topper. Is Bobby a little boy? Is he a member of your family?"

"No. Bobby lives next door. He's twelve. He teases me. He pulls my hair, and he tore my dress. He put mud in my shoes and he hit Topper with a rock." Her eyes widened alarmingly. "Mommy!" she screamed. *"Mommy!"*

The sound was so electrifying that George Smollett jumped out of his chair. Dr. Frohlich waved him back.

"What happened, Julia? Why are you calling your mother? What's happened to Bobby?"

"He's killed him! He's killed him!" the ten-year-old voice shrieked.

"Who?" Frohlich said loudly. "Who?"

"I warned him," Julia sobbed, her shoulders shaking. "I told him what I would do. I told him!"

Again, with startling suddenness, the sobs ceased. The woman's body stiffened in the chair, and her thin arms folded themselves across her chest. But the real transformation was in her eyes; a metamorphosis to something ageless and yet ancient, a craftiness, a terrifying cunning.

"Sic 'em," the girl-voice whispered. "Sic 'em Topper! Kill him! *Kill him!*"

"Oh, my God," George said aloud.

"Please!" Frohlich motioned angrily. "Julia, listen to me. I want you to calm down. I want you to explain everything to me, very clearly. Did you set your dog on Bobby? Did you tell your dog to hurt Bobby?"

Her body sagged. She nodded.

"Did he hurt Bobby? Did Topper kill him?"

"No," she said faintly. "He hurt Bobby. He didn't kill him. He hurt Bobby in the neck. But they killed Topper. They killed my dog. And it's my fault. My fault . . ."

Her voice faded, died.

Frohlich looked sharply towards the husband. "Please leave now, Mr. Smollett. I think you should leave for a while."

George blew air out of his mouth, and went to the door.

Fifteen minutes later, the blinds had been opened, and the whole episode seemed like a dream of long ago. Dr. Frohlich, now a solid, very human figure behind the desk, beamed at them with pure professional pleasure.

"So, Mrs. Smollett. Now you know. It was this one incident of your childhood—this one small tragedy of your past innocence which is responsible for your problem. More than anything, you have a strong feeling of guilt. You blame yourself for what happened to little Bobby, when, in all likelihood, you were not in any way at fault. But you wished that Topper would turn on him, and then you saw your wish become reality. So—you accused yourself of the crime. And by that accusation, you've condemned yourself to a terror that you needn't ever have again."

He looked towards the window. "Well, the sun's out. I think that's symbolic, Julia. Don't you?"

She smiled at him.

Three weeks later, the telephone was ringing in the foyer when Julia Smollett returned from the morning's shopping tour. She hurried to answer it.

"Mrs. Smollett? This is Dr. Frohlich."

"Oh, hello, Doctor! It's nice to hear from you."

"I just thought I'd find out what's doing up there. Seems to me we had an appointment yesterday. Did you forget it?"

"Oh, my goodness! It went clean out of my head!"

He laughed heartily. "Well! We'll have to find the answer to that little block. But maybe it's not so hard to understand. Maybe you're just feeling too well—"

"I think you're right," she said. "I haven't felt so well in years. You really cured me—of my, you know, fears. Why, I actually like Attila!"

"Attila? Is that what you call that animal?"

"It was George's idea. I'm used to it by now."

"Well, I just thought I would remind you. Suppose you come by the same time next week?"

"Fine, Doctor Frohlich."

She hung up the phone. Then she went up the carpeted stairs to the second-floor bedroom.

Alice, the maid, was straightening up in George's room when Julia entered. She was standing at the window, looking at the back lawn where the dog lay quietly beneath the only tree.

"You goin' out to the dog, Mis' Smollett?"

"Why, yes, Alice. Why?"

"I dunno, Mis' Smollett. I wouldn't trust that there animal. He's a killer dog if I ever saw one."

"Oh, Alice!"

"I'm serious, Mis' Smollett. You 'member what I told you. That dog'll kill somebody someday."

She went out muttering. Julia waited until she was gone, and then slid back the walnut door of her husband's closet, reaching for his favorite tweed jacket with the leather patches on the elbows. She slipped it off the hanger and threw it over her arm.

Then she returned downstairs and went out to the back lawn.

It was a lovely day. Attila was waiting patiently, his jaws spread in a grin, his red tongue oscillating, his great teeth gleaming.

Julia patted the huge head, and then brought the jacket out from behind her back.

"Sic 'em!" she said fiercely, pushing the George-smell in the dog's nostrils. "Sic 'em, Attila!"

SLIME

Joseph Payne Brennan

IT WAS A GREAT GRAY-BLACK HOOD OF HORROR MOVING over the floor of the sea. It slid through the soft ooze like a monstrous mantle of slime obscenely animated with questing life. It was by turns viscid and fluid. At times it flattened out and flowed through the carpet of mud like an inky pool; occasionally it paused, seeming to shrink in upon itself, and reared up out of the ooze until it resembled an irregular cone or a gigantic hood. Although it possessed no eyes, it had a marvelously developed sense of touch, and it possessed a sensitivity to minute vibrations which was almost akin to telepathy. It was plastic, essentially shapeless. It could shoot out long tentacles, until it bore a resemblance to a nightmare squid or a huge starfish; it could retract itself into a round flattened disk, or squeeze into an irregular hunched shape so that it looked like a black boulder sunk on the bottom of the sea.

It had prowled the black water endlessly. It had been formed when the earth and the seas were young; it was almost as old as the ocean itself. It moved through a night which had no beginning and no dissolution. The black sea basin where it lurked had been dark since the world began —an environment only a little less inimical than the stupendous gulfs of interplanetary space.

It was animated by a single, unceasing, never-satisfied drive: a voracious, insatiable hunger. It could survive for months without food, but minutes after eating it was as ravenous as ever. Its appetite was appalling and incalculable.

On the icy ink-black floor of the sea the battle for survival was savage, hideous—and usually brief. But for the shape of moving slime there was no battle. It ate whatever came its way, regardless of size, shape or disposition. It absorbed microscopic plankton and giant squid with equal assurance. Had its surface been less fluid, it might have retained the circular scars left by the grappling suckers of the wildly threshing deep-water squid, or the jagged toothmarks of the anachronistic frillshark, but as it was, neither left any evidence of its absorption. When the lifting curtain of living slime swayed out of the mud and closed upon them, their fiercest death throes came to nothing.

The horror did not know fear. There was nothing to be afraid of. It ate whatever moved, or tried not to move, and it had never encountered anything which could in turn eat it. If a squid's sucker, or a shark's tooth, tore into the mass of its viscosity, the rent flowed in upon itself and immediately closed. If a segment was detached, it could be retrieved and absorbed back into the whole.

The black mantle reigned supreme in its savage world of slime and silence. It groped greedily and endlessly through the mud, eating and never sleeping, never resting. If it lay still, it was only to trap food which might otherwise be lost. If it rushed with terrifying speed across the slimy bottom, it was never to escape an enemy, but always to flop its hideous fluidity upon its sole and inevitable quarry—food.

It had evolved out of the muck and slime of the primitive sea floor, and it was as alien to ordinary terrestrial life as the weird denizens of some wild planet in a distant galaxy. It was an anachronistic experiment of nature compared to which the saber-toothed tiger, the woolly mammoth and even Tyrannosaurus, the slashing, murderous king of the great earth reptiles, were as tame, weak entities.

Had it not been for a vast volcanic upheaval on the bottom of the ocean basin, the black horror would have crept out its entire existence on the silent sea ooze without ever manifesting its hideous powers to mankind.

Fate, in the form of a violent subterranean explosion, covering huge areas of the ocean's floor, hurled it out of its black slime world and sent it spinning toward the surface.

Had it been an ordinary deep-water fish, it never would have survived the experience. The explosion itself, or the drastic lessening of water pressure as it shot toward the surface, would have destroyed it. But it was no ordinary fish. Its viscosity, or plasticity, or whatever it was that constituted its essentially amoebic structure, permitted it to survive.

It reached the surface slightly stunned and flopped on the surging waters like a great blob of black blubber. Immense waves stirred up by the subterranean explosion swept it swiftly toward shore, and because it was somewhat stunned, it did not try to resist the roaring mountains of water.

Along with scattered ash, pumice and the puffed bodies of dead fish, the black horror was hurled toward a beach. The huge waves carried it more than a mile inland, far beyond the strip of sandy shore, and deposited it in the midst of a deep brackish swamp area.

As luck would have it, the submarine explosion and subsequent tidal wave took place at night, and therefore the slime horror was not immediately subjected to a new and hateful experience—light.

Although the midnight darkness of the storm-lashed swamp did not begin to compare with the stygian blackness of the sea bottom, where even violet rays of the spectrum could not penetrate, the marsh darkness was nevertheless deep and intense.

As the water of the great wave receded, sluicing through the thorn jungle and back out to sea, the black horror clung to a mud bank surrounded by a rank growth of cattails. It was aware of the sudden, startling change in its environment and for some time it lay motionless, concentrating its attention on obscure internal readjustment which the absence of crushing pressure and a surrounding cloak of frigid seawater demanded. Its adaptability was incredible and horrifying. It achieved in a few hours what an ordinary creature could have attained only through a process of gradual evolution. Three hours after the titanic wave flopped it onto the mudbank, it had undergone swift organic changes which left it relatively at ease in its new environment.

In fact, it felt lighter and more mobile than it ever had before in its sea-basin existence.

As it flung out feelers and attuned itself to the minutest vibrations and emanations of the swamp area, its pristine hunger drive reasserted itself with overwhelmng urgency. And the tale which its sensory apparatus returned to the monstrous something which served it as a brain, excited it tremendously. It sensed at once that the swamp was filled with luscious tidbits of quivering food—more food, and food of a greater variety than it had ever encountered on the cold floor of the sea.

Its savage, incessant hunger seemed unbearable. Its slimy mass was swept by a shuddering wave of anticipation.

Sliding off the mud bank, it slithered over the cattails into an adjacent area consisting of deep black pools interspersed with water-logged tussocks. Weed stalks stuck up out of the water and the decayed trunks of fallen trees floated half-submerged in the larger pools.

Ravenous with hunger, it sloshed into the bog area, flicking its fluid tentacles about. Within minutes it had snatched up several fat frogs and a number of small fish. These, however, merely titillated its appetite. Its hunger turned into a kind of ecstatic fury. It commenced a systematic hunt, plunging to the bottom of each pool and quickly but carefully exploring every inch of its oozy bottom. The first creature of any size which it encountered was a muskrat. An immense curtain of adhesive slime suddenly swept out of the darkness, closed upon it—and squeezed.

Heartened and whetted by its find, the hood of horror rummaged the rank pools with renewed zeal. When it surfaced, it carefully probed the tussocks for anything that might have escaped it in the water. Once it snatched up a small bird nesting in some swamp grass. Occasionally it slithered up the criss-crossed trunks of fallen trees, bearing them down with its unspeakable slimy bulk, and hung briefly suspended like a great dripping curtain of black marsh mud.

It was approaching a somewhat less swampy and more deeply wooded area when it gradually became aware of a subtle change in its new environment. It paused, hesitating, and remained half in and half out of a small pond near the edge of the nearest trees.

Although it had absorbed twenty-five or thirty pounds of food in the form of frogs, fish, water snakes, the muskrat and a few smaller creatures, its fierce hunger had not left it. Its monstrous appetite urged it on, and yet something held it anchored in the pond.

What it sensed, but could not literally see, was the rising sun spreading a gray light over the swamp. The horror had never encountered any illumination except that generated by the grotesque phosphorescent appendages of various deep-sea fishes. Natural light was totally unknown to it.

As the dawn light strengthened, breaking through the scattering storm clouds, the black slime monster fresh from the inky floor of the sea sensed that something utterly unknown was flooding in upon it. Light was hateful to it. It cast out quick feelers, hoping to catch and crush the light. But the more frenzied its efforts became, the more intense became the abhorred aura surrounding it.

At length, as the sun rose visibly above the trees, the horror, in baffled rage rather than in fear, grudgingly slid back into the pond and burrowed into the soft ooze of its bottom. There it remained while the sun shone and the small creatures of the swamp ventured forth on furtive errands.

A few miles away from Wharton's Swamp, in the small town of Clinton Center, Henry Hossing sleepily crawled out of the improvised alley shack which had afforded him a degree of shelter for the night and stumbled into the street. Passing a hand across his rheumy eyes, he scratched the stubble on his cheek and blinked listlessly at the rising sun. He had not slept well; the storm of the night before had kept him awake. Besides he had gone to bed hungry, and that never agreed with him.

Glancing furtively along the street, he walked slouched forward, with his head bent down, and most of the time he kept his eyes on the walk or on the gutter in the hopes of spotting a chance coin.

Clinton Center had not been kind to him. The handouts were sparse, and only yesterday he had been warned out of town by one of the local policemen.

Grumbling to himself, he reached the end of the street and started to cross. Suddenly he stopped quickly and snatched up something from the edge of the pavement.

It was a crumpled green bill, and as he frantically unfolded it, a look of stupefied rapture spread across his bristly face. Ten dollars! More money than he had possessed at any one time in months!

Stowing it carefully in the one good pocket of his seedy gray jacket, he crossed the street with a swift stride. Instead of sweeping the sidewalks, his eye now darted along the rows of stores and restaurants.

He paused at one restaurant, hesitated, and finally went on until he found another less pretentious one a few blocks away.

When he sat down, the counterman shook his head. "Get goin', bud. No free coffee today."

With a wide grin, the hobo produced his ten-dollar bill and spread it on the counter. "That covers a good breakfast here, pardner?"

The counterman seemed irritated. "OK. OK. What'll you have?" He eyed the bill suspiciously.

Henry Hossing ordered orange juice, toast, ham and eggs, oatmeal, melon and coffee.

When it appeared, he ate every bit of it, ordered three additional cups of coffee, paid the check as if two-dollar breakfasts were customary with him, and then sauntered back to the street.

Shortly after noon, after his three-dollar lunch, he saw the liquor store. For a few minutes he stood across the street from it, fingering his five-dollar bill. Finally he crossed with an abstracted smile, entered and bought a quart of rye.

He hesitated on the sidewalk, debating whether or not he should return to the little shack in the side alley. After a minute or two of indecision, he decided against it and struck out instead for Wharton's Swamp. The local police were far less likely to disturb him there, and since the skies were clearing and the weather mild, there was little immediate need of shelter.

Angling off the highway which skirted the swamp several miles from town, he crossed a marshy meadow, pushed through a fringe of brush and sat down under a sweet-gum tree which bordered a deeply wooded area.

By late afternoon he had achieved a quite cheerful glow, and he had little inclination to return to Clinton Center. Rousing himself from reverie, he stumbled about collecting enough wood for a small fire and went back to his sylvan seat under the sweet-gum.

He slept briefly as dusk descended, but finally bestirred himself again to build a fire, as deeper shadows fell over the swamp. Then he returned to his swiftly diminishing bottle. He was suspended in a warm net of inflamed fantasy when something abruptly broke the spell and brought him back to earth.

The flickering flames of his fire had dwindled down until now only a dim eerie glow illuminated the immediate area under the sweet-gum. He saw nothing and at the moment heard nothing, and yet he was filled with a sudden and profound sense of lurking menace.

He stood up, staggering, leaned back against the sweet-gum and peered fearfully into the shadows. In the deep darkness beyond the waning arc of firelight he could distinguish nothing which had any discernible form or color.

Then he detected the stench and shuddered. In spite of the reek of cheap whiskey which clung around him, the smell was overpowering. It was heavy, fulsome, fetid, alien and utterly repellent. It was vaguely fishlike, but otherwise beyond any known comparison.

As he stood trembling under the sweet-gum, Henry Hossing thought of something dead which had lain for long ages at the bottom of the sea.

Filled with mounting alarm, he looked around for some wood which he might add to the dying fire. All he could find nearby however were a few twigs. He threw these on and the flames licked up briefly and subsided.

He listened and heard—or imagined he heard—an odd

sort of slithering sound in the nearby bushes. It seemed to retreat slightly as the flames shot up.

Genuine terror took possession of him. He knew that he was in no condition to flee—and now he came to the horrifying conclusion that whatever unspeakable menace waited in the surrounding darkness was temporarily held at bay only by the failing gleam of his little fire.

Frantically he looked around for more wood. But there was none. None, that is, within the faint glow of firelight. And he dared not venture beyond.

He began to tremble uncontrollably. He tried to scream but no sound came out of tightened throat.

The ghastly stench became stronger, and now he was sure that he could hear a strange sliding, slithering sound in the black shadows beyond the remaining spark of firelight.

He stood frozen in absolute helpless panic as the tiny fire smoldered down into darkness.

At the last instant, a charred bit of wood broke apart, sending up a few sparks, and in that flicker of final light he glimpsed the horror.

It had already glided out of the bushes and now it rushed across the small clearing with nightmare speed. It was a final incarnation of all the fears, shuddering apprehensions and bad dreams which Henry Hossing had ever known in his life. It was a fiend from the pit of Hell come to claim him at last.

A terrible ringing scream burst from his throat, but it was smothered before it was finished as the black shape of slime fastened upon him with irresistible force.

Giles Gowse—"Old Man" Gowse—got out of bed after eight hours of fitful tossing and intermittent nightmares and grouchily brewed coffee in the kitchen of his dilapidated farmhouse on the edge of Wharton's Swamp. Half the night, it seemed, the stench of stale seawater had permeated the house. His interrupted sleep had been full of foreboding, full of shadowy and evil portents.

Muttering to himself, he finished breakfast, took a milk

pail from the pantry and started for the barn where he kept his single cow.

As he approached the barn, the strange offensive odor which had plagued him during the night assailed his nostrils anew.

"Wharton's Swamp! That's what it is!" he told himself. And he shook his fist at it.

When he entered the barn, the stench was stronger than ever. Scowling, he strode toward the rickety stall where he kept the cow, Sarey.

Then he stood still and stared. Sarey was gone. The stall was empty.

He reentered the barnyard. "Sarey!" he called.

Rushing back into the barn, he inspected the stall. The rancid reek of the sea was strong here and now he noticed a kind of shine on the floor. Bending closer, he saw that it was a slick coat of glistening slime, as if some unspeakable creature covered with ooze had crept in and out of the stall.

This discovery, coupled with the weird disappearance of Sarey, was too much for his jangled nerves. With a wild yell he ran out of the barn and started for Clinton Center, two miles away.

His reception in the town enraged him. When he tried to tell people about the disappearance of his cow, Sarey, about the reek of sea and ooze in his barn the night before, they laughed at him. The more impolite ones, that is. Most of the others patiently heard him out—and then winked and touched their heads significantly when he was out of sight.

One man, the druggist, Jim Jelinson, seemed mildly interested. He said that, as he was coming through his backyard from the garage late the previous evening, he had heard a fearful shriek somewhere in the distant darkness. It might, he averred, have come from the direction of Wharton's Swamp. But it had not been repeated and eventually he had dismissed it from his mind.

When Old Man Gowse started for home late in the afternoon he was filled with sullen, resentful bitterness. They thought he was crazy, eh? Well, Sarey *was* gone; they couldn't explain *that* away, could they? They explained the smell by saying it was dead fish cast up by the big wave which had washed into the swamp during the storm. Well —maybe. And the slime on his barn floor they said was snails. *Snails!* As if any he'd ever seen could cause that much slime!

As he was nearing home, he met Rupert Barnaby, his nearest neighbor. Rupert was carrying a rifle and he was accompanied by Jibbe, his hound.

Although there had been an element of bad blood between the two bachelor neighbors for some time, Old Man Gowse, much to Barnaby's surprise, nodded and stopped.

"Evenin' hunt, neighbor?"

Barnaby nodded. "Thought Jibbe might start up a coon. Moon later, likely."

"My cow's gone," Old Man Gowse said abruptly. "If you should see her—" He paused. "But I don't think you will. . . ."

Barnaby, bewildered, stared at him. "What you gettin' at?"

Old Man Gowse repeated what he had been telling all day in Clinton Center.

He shook his head when he finished, adding. "I wouldn't go huntin' in that swamp tonight fur—ten thousand dollars!"

Rupert Barnaby threw back his head and laughed. He was a big man, muscular, resourceful and level-headed— little given to even mild flights of the imagination.

"Gowse," he laughed, "no use you givin' me those spook stories! Your cow just got loose and wandered off. Why, I ain't even seen a bobcat in that swamp for over a year!"

Old Man Gowse set his lips in a grim line. "Maybe," he said, as he turned away, "you'll see suthin' worse than a wildcat in that swamp tonight!"

Shaking his head, Barnaby took off after his impatient hound. Old Man Gowse was getting queer all right. One of these days he'd probably go off altogether and have to be locked up.

Jibbe ran ahead, sniffing, darting from one ditch to another. As twilight closed in, Barnaby angled off the main road onto a twisting path which led into Wharton's Swamp.

He loved hunting. He would rather tramp through the brush than sit home in an easy chair. And even if an evening's foray turned up nothing, he didn't particularly mind. Actually he made out quite well; at least half his meat supply consisted of the rabbits, racoons and occasional deer which he brought down in Wharton's Swamp.

When the moon rose, he was deep in the swamp. Twice Jibbe started off after rabbits, but both times he returned quickly, looking somewhat sheepish.

Something about his actions began to puzzle Barnaby. The dog seemed reluctant to move ahead; he hung directly in front of the hunter. Once Barnaby tripped over him and nearly fell headlong.

The hunter paused finally, frowning, and looked ahead. The swamp appeared no different than usual. True, a rather offensive stench hung over it, but that was merely the result of the big waves which had splashed far inland during the recent storm. Probably an accumulation of seaweed and the decaying bodies of some dead fish lay rotting in the stagnant pools of the swamp.

Barnaby spoke sharply to the dog. "What ails you, boy? Git now! You trip me again, you'll get a boot!"

The dog started ahead some distance, but with an air of reluctance. He sniffed the clumps of marsh grass in a perfunctory manner and seemed to have lost interest in the hunt.

Barnaby grew exasperated. Even when they discovered the fresh track of a racoon in the soft mud near a little pool, Jibbe manifested only slight interest.

He did run on ahead a little further however, and Barnaby began to hope that, as they closed in, he would regain his customary enthusiasm.

In this he was mistaken. As they approached a thickly wooded area, latticed with tree thorns and covered with a heavy growth of cattails, the dog suddenly crouched in the shadows and refused to budge.

Barnaby was sure that the racoon had taken refuge in

the nearby thickets. The dog's unheard-of conduct infuriated him.

After a number of sharp cuffs, Jibbe arose stiffly and moved ahead, the hair on his neck bristled up like a lion's mane.

Swearing to himself, Barnaby pushed into the darkened thickets after him.

It was quite black under the trees, in spite of the moonlight, and he moved cautiously in order to avoid stepping into a pool.

Suddenly, with a frantic yelp of terror, Jibbe literally darted between his legs and shot out of the thickets. He ran on, howling weirdly as he went.

For the first time that evening Barnaby experienced a thrill of fear. In all his previous experience, Jibbe had never turned tail. On one occasion he had even plunged in after a sizable bear.

Scowling into the deep darkness, Barnaby could see nothing. There were no baleful eyes glaring at him.

As his own eyes tried to penetrate the surrounding blackness, he recalled Old Man Gowse's warning with a bitter grimace. If the old fool happened to spot Jibbe streaking out of the swamp, Barnaby would never hear the end of it.

The thought of this angered him. He pushed ahead now with a feeling of sullen rage for whatever had terrified the dog. A good rifle shot would solve the mystery.

All at once he stopped and listened. From the darkness immediately ahead, he detected an odd sound, as if a large bulk were being dragged over the cattails.

He hesitated, unable to see anything, stoutly resisting an idiotic impulse to flee. The black darkness and the slimy stench of stagnant pools here in the thickets seemed to be suffocating him.

His heart began to pound as the slithering noise came closer. Every instinct told him to turn and run, but a kind of desperate stubbornness held him rooted to the spot.

The sound grew louder, and suddenly he was positive that something deadly and formidable was rushing toward him through the thickets with accelerated speed.

Throwing up his rifle, he pointed at the direction of the sound and fired.

In the brief flash of the rifle he saw something black and enormous and glistening, like a great flapping hood, break through the final thicket. It seemed to be *rolling* toward him, and it was moving with nightmare swiftness.

He wanted to scream and run, but even as the horror rushed forward, he understood that flight at this point would be futile. Even though the blood seemed to have congealed in his veins, he held the rifle pointed up and kept on firing.

The shots had no more visible effect than so many pebbles launched from a slingshot. At the last instant his nerve broke and he tried to escape, but the monstrous hood lunged upon him, flapped over him and squeezed, and his attempt at a scream turned into a tiny gurgle in his throat.

Old Man Gowse got up early, after another uneasy night, and walked out to inspect the barnyard area. Nothing further seemed amiss, but there was still no sign of Sarey. And that detestable odor arose from the direction of Wharton's Swamp when the wind was right.

After breakfast, Gowse set out for Rupert Barnaby's place, a mile or so distant along the road. He wasn't sure himself what he expected to find.

When he reached Barnaby's small but neat frame house, all was quiet. Too quiet. Usually Barnaby was up and about soon after sunrise.

On a sudden impulse, Gowse walked up the path and rapped on the front door. He waited and there was no reply. He knocked again, and after another pause, stepped off the porch.

Jibbe, Barnaby's hound, slunk around the side of the house. Ordinarily he would bound about and bark. But today he stood motionless—or nearly so—he was trembling—and stared at Gowse. The dog had a cowed, frightened, guilty air which was entirely alien to him.

"Where's Rup?" Gowse called to him. "Go get Rup!"

Instead of starting off, the dog threw back his head and emitted an eerie, long-drawn howl.

Gowse shivered. With a backward glance at the silent house, he started off down the road.

Now maybe they'd listen to him, he thought grimly. The day before they had laughed about the disappearance of Sarey. Maybe they wouldn't laugh so easily when he told them that Rupert Barnaby had gone into Wharton's Swamp with his dog—and that the dog had come back alone!

When Police Chief Miles Underbeck saw Old Man Gowse come into headquarters in Clinton Center, he sat back and sighed heavily. He was busy this morning and undoubtedly Old Man Gowse was coming in to inquire about that infernal cow of his that had wandered off.

The old eccentric had a new and startling report, however. He claimed that Rupert Barnaby was missing. He'd gone into the swamp the night before, Gowse insisted, and had not returned.

When Chief Underbeck questioned him closely, Gowse admitted that he wasn't *positive* Barnaby hadn't returned. It was barely possible that he had returned home very early in the morning and then left again before Gowse arrived.

But Gowse fixed his flashing eyes on the Chief and shook his head. "He never came out, I tell ye! That dog of his knows! Howled, he did, like a dog howls for the dead! Whatever come took Sarey—got Barnaby in the swamp last night!"

Chief Underbeck was not an excitable man. Gowse's burst of melodrama irritated him and left him unimpressed.

Somewhat gruffly he promised to look into the matter if Barnaby had not turned up by evening. Barnaby, he pointed out, knew the swamp better than anyone else in the county. And he was perfectly capable of taking care of himself. Probably, the Chief suggested, he had sent the dog home and gone elsewhere after finishing his hunt the evening before. The chances were he'd be back by suppertime.

Old Man Gowse shook his head with a kind of fatalistic skepticism. Vouching that events would soon prove his fears well founded, he shambled grouchily out of the station.

The day passed and there was no sign of Rupert Barnaby. At six o'clock, Old Man Gowse grimly marched into the Crown, Clinton Center's second-rung hotel, and registered for a room. At seven o'clock Chief Underbeck dispatched a prowl car to Barnaby's place. He waited impatiently for its return, drumming on the desk, disinterestedly shuffling through a sheaf of reports which had accumulated during the day.

The prowl car returned shortly before eight. Sergeant Grimes made his report. "Nobody there, sir. Place locked up tight. Searched the grounds. All we saw was Barnaby's dog. Howled and ran off as if the devil were on his tail!"

Chief Underbeck was troubled. If Barnaby *was* missing, a search should be started at once. But it was already getting dark, and portions of Wharton's Swamp were very nearly impassable even during the day. Besides, there was no proof that Barnaby had not gone off for a visit, perhaps to nearby Stantonville, for instance, to call on a crony and stay overnight.

By nine o'clock he had decided to postpone any action till morning. A search now would probably be futile in any case. The swamp offered too many obstacles. If Barnaby had not turned up by morning, and there was no report that he had been seen elsewhere, a systematic search of the marsh could begin.

Not long after he had arrived at this decision, and as he was somewhat wearily preparing to leave Headquarters and go home, a new and genuinely alarming interruption took place.

Shortly before nine-thirty, a car braked to a sudden stop outside Headquarters. An elderly man hurried in, supporting by the arm a sobbing, hysterical young girl. Her skirt and stockings were torn and there were a number of scratches on her face.

After assisting her to a chair, the man turned to Chief Underbeck and the other officers who gathered around.

"Picked her up on the highway out near Wharton's Swamp. Screaming at the top of her lungs!" He wiped his forehead. "She ran right in front of my car. Missed her by a miracle. She was so crazy with fear I couldn't make sense out of what she said. Seems like something grabbed her boy friend in the bushes out there. Anyway, I got her in the car without much trouble and I guess I broke a speed law getting here."

Chief Underbeck surveyed the man keenly. He was obviously shaken himself, and since he did not appear to be concealing anything, the Chief turned to the girl.

He spoke soothingly, doing his best to reassure her, and at length she composed herself sufficiently to tell her story.

Her name was Dolores Rell and she lived in nearby Stantonville. Earlier in the evening she had gone riding with her fiancé, Jason Bukmeist of Clinton Center. As Jason was driving along the highway adjacent to Wharton's Swamp, she had remarked that the early evening moonlight looked very romantic over the marsh. Jason had stopped the car, and after they had surveyed the scene for some minutes, he suggested that since the evening was warm, a brief "stroll in the moonlight" might be fun.

Dolores had been reluctant to leave the car, but at length had been persuaded to take a short walk along the edge of the marsh where the terrain was relatively firm.

As the couple were walking along under the trees, perhaps twenty yards or so from the car, Dolores became aware of an unpleasant odor and wanted to turn back. Jason, however, told her she only imagined it and insisted on going farther. As the trees grew closer together, they walked Indian file, Jason taking the lead.

Suddenly, she said, they both heard something swishing through the brush toward them. Jason told her not to be frightened, that it was probably someone's cow. As it came closer, however, it seemed to be moving with incredible speed. And it didn't seem to be making the kind of noise a cow would make.

At the last second Jason whirled with a cry of fear and told her to run. Before she could move, she saw a monstrous something rushing under the trees in the dim moonlight. For an instant she stood rooted with horror; then she turned and ran. She thought she heard Jason running be-

hind her. She couldn't be sure. But immediately after, she
heard him scream.

In spite of her terror, she turned and looked behind her.

At this point in her story she became hysterical again
and several minutes passed before she could go on.

She could not describe exactly what she had seen as she
looked over her shoulder. The thing which she had glimpsed
rushing under the trees had caught up with Jason. It
almost completely covered him. All she could see of him
was his agonized face and part of one arm, low near the
ground, as if the thing were squatting astride him. She
could not say what it was. It was black, formless, bestial
and yet not bestial. It was the dark gliding kind of indescribable horror which she had shuddered at when she was
a little girl alone in the nursery at night.

She shuddered now and covered her eyes as she tried to
picture what she had seen. "O God—*the darkness came
alive! The darkness came alive!"*

Somehow, she went on presently, she had stumbled
through the trees into the road. She was so terrified she
hardly noticed the approaching car.

There could be no doubt that Dolores Rell was in the
grip of genuine terror. Chief Underbeck acted with alacri-
ty. After the white-faced girl had been driven to a nearby
hospital for treatment of her scratches and the administra-
tion of a sedative, Underbeck rounded up all available men
on the force, equipped them with shotguns, rifles and flashlights, hurried them into four prowl cars and started off for
Wharton's Swamp.

Jason Bukmeist's car was found where he had parked it.
It had not been disturbed. A search of the nearby swamp
area, conducted in the glare of flashlights, proved fruitless.
Whatever had attacked Bukmeist had apparently carried
him off into the farthest recesses of the sprawling swamp.

After two futile hours of brush breaking and marsh
sloshing, Chief Underbeck wearily rounded up his men
and called off the hunt until morning.

As the first faint streaks of dawn appeared in the sky
over Wharton's Swamp, the search began again. Reinforce-
ments, including civilian volunteers from Clinton Center,

had arrived, and a systematic combing of the entire swamp commenced.

By noon, the search had proved fruitless—or nearly so. One of the searchers brought in a battered hat and a rye whiskey bottle which he had discovered on the edge of the marsh under a sweet-gum tree. The shapeless felt hat was old and worn, but it was dry. It had, therefore, apparently been discarded in the swamp since the storm of a few days ago. The whiskey bottle looked new; in fact, a few drops of rye remained in it. The searcher reported that the remains of a small campfire were also found under the sweet-gum.

In the hope that this evidence might have some bearing on the disappearance of Jason Bukmeist, Chief Underbeck ordered a canvass of every liquor store in Clinton Center in an attempt to learn the names of everyone who had recently purchased a bottle of the particular brand of rye found under the tree.

The search went on, and midafternoon brought another, more ominous discovery. A diligent searcher, investigating a trampled area in a large growth of cattails, picked a rifle out of the mud.

After the slime and dirt had been wiped away, two of the searchers vouched that it belonged to Rupert Barnaby. One of them had hunted with him and remembered a bit of scrollwork on the rifle stock.

While Chief Underbeck was weighing this unpalatable bit of evidence, a report of the liquor store canvass in Clinton Center arrived. Every recent purchaser of a quart bottle of the particular brand in question had been investigated. Only one could not be located—a tramp who had hung around the town for several days and had been ordered out.

By evening most of the exhausted searching party were convinced that the tramp, probably in a state of homicidal viciousness brought on by drink, had murdered both Rupert Barnaby and Jason and secreted their bodies in one of the deep pools of the swamp. The chances were the murderer was still sleeping off the effects of drink somewhere in the tangled thickets of the marsh.

Most of the searchers regarded Dolores Rell's melodramatic story with a great deal of skepticism. In the dim moonlight, they pointed out, a frenzied, wild-eyed tramp bent on imminent murder might very well have resembled some kind of monster. And the girl's hysteria had probably magnified what she had seen.

As night closed over the dismal morass, Chief Underbeck reluctantly suspended the hunt. In view of the fact that the murderer probably still lurked in the woods, however, he decided to establish a system of night-long patrols along the highway which paralleled the swamp. If the quarry lay hidden in the treacherous tangle of trees and brush, he would not be able to escape onto the highway without running into one of the patrols. The only other means of egress from the swamp lay miles across the mire where the open sea washed against a reedy beach. And it was quite unlikely that the fugitive would even attempt escape in that direction.

The patrols were established in three-hour shifts, two men to a patrol, both heavily armed and both equipped with powerful searchlights. They were ordered to investigate every sound or movement which they detected in the brush bordering the highway. After a single command to halt, they were to shoot to kill. Any curious motorists who stopped to inquire about the hunt were to be swiftly waved on their way, after being warned not to give rides to anyone and to report all hitchhikers.

Fred Storr and Luke Matson, on the midnight-to-three o'clock patrol, passed an uneventful two hours on their particular stretch of the highway. Matson finally sat down on a fallen tree stump a few yards from the edge of the road.

"Legs givin' out," he commented wryly, resting his rifle on the stump. "Might as well sit a few minutes."

Fred Storr lingered nearby. "Guess so, Luke. Don't look like—" Suddenly he scowled into the black fringe of the swamp. "You hear something, Luke?"

Luke listened, twisting around on the stump. "Well, maybe," he said finally, "kind of a little scratchy sound like."

He got up, retrieving his rifle.

"Let's take a look," Fred suggested in a low voice. He stepped over the stump and Luke followed him toward the tangle of brush which marked the border of the swamp jungle.

Several yards farther along they stopped again. The sound became more audible. It was a kind of slithering, scraping sound, such as might be produced by a heavy body dragging itself over uneven ground.

"Sounds like—a snake," Luke ventured. "A damn big snake!"

"We'll get a little closer," Fred whispered. "You be ready with that gun when I switch on my light!"

They moved ahead a few more yards. Then a powerful yellow ray stabbed into the thickets ahead as Fred switched on his flashlight. The ray searched the darkness, probing in one direction and then another.

Luke lowered his rifle a little, frowning. "Don't see a thing," he said. "Nothing but a big pool of black scum up ahead there."

Before Fred had time to reply, the pool of black scum reared up into horrible life. In one hideous second it hunched itself into an unspeakable glistening hood and rolled forward with fearful speed.

Luke Matson screamed and fired simultaneously as the monstrous scarf of slime shot forward. A moment later it swayed above him. He fired again and the thing fell upon him.

In avoiding the initial rush of the horror, Fred Storr lost his footing. He fell headlong—and turned just in time to witness a sight which slowed the blood in his veins.

The monster had pounced upon Luke Matson. Now, as Fred watched, literally paralyzed with horror, it spread itself over and around the form of Luke until he was completely enveloped. The faint writhing of his limbs could still be seen. Then the thing squeezed, swelling into a hood and flattening itself again, and the writhing ceased.

As soon as the thing lifted and swung forward in his direction, Fred Storr, goaded by frantic fear, overcame the paralysis of horror which had frozen him.

Grabbing the rifle which had fallen beside him, he aimed

it at the shape of living slime and started firing. Pure terror possessed him as he saw that the shots were having no effect. The thing lunged toward him, to all visible appearances entirely oblivious to the rifle slugs tearing into its loathsome viscid mass.

Acting out of some instinct which he himself could not have named, Fred Storr dropped the rifle and seized his flashlight, playing its powerful beam directly upon the onrushing horror.

The thing stopped, scant feet away, and appeared to hesitate. It slid quickly aside at an angle, but he followed it immediately with the cone of light. It backed up finally and flattened out, as if trying by that means to avoid the light, but he trained the beam on it steadily, sensing with every primitive fiber which he possessed that the yellow shaft of light was the one thing which held off hideous death.

Now there were shouts in the nearby darkness and other lights began stabbing the shadows. Members of the adjacent patrols, alarmed by the sound of rifle fire, had come running to investigate.

Suddenly the nameless horror squirmed quickly out of the flashlight's beam and rushed away in the darkness.

In the leaden light of early dawn, Chief Underbeck climbed into a police car waiting on the highway near Wharton's Swamp and headed back for Clinton Center. He had made a decision and he was grimly determined to act on it at once.

When he reached Headquarters, he made two telephone calls in quick succession, one to the governor of the state and the other to the commander of the nearby Camp Evans Military Reservation.

The horror in Wharton's Swamp—he had decided—could not be coped with by the limited men and resources at his command.

Rupert Barnaby, Jason Bukmeist and Luke Matson had without any doubt perished in the swamp. The anonymous tramp, it now began to appear, far from being the murderer, had been only one more victim. And Fred Storr—well, he hadn't disappeared. But the other patrol members had found him sitting on the ground near the edge of the swamp in the clutches of a mind-warping fear which had, temporarily at least, reduced him to near idiocy. Hours after he had been taken home and put to bed, he had refused to loosen his grip on a flashlight which he squeezed in one hand. When they switched the flashlight off, he screamed, and they had to switch it on again. His story was so wildly melodramatic it could scarcely be accepted by rational minds. And yet—they had said as much about Dolores Rell's hysterical account. And Fred Storr was no excitable young girl; he had a reputation for level-headedness, stolidity and verbal honesty which was touched with understatement rather than exaggeration. As Chief Underbeck arose and walked out to his car in order to start back to Wharton's Swamp, he noticed Old Man Gowse coming down the block.

With a sudden thrill of horror he remembered the eccentric's missing cow. Before the old man came abreast, he slammed the car door and issued crisp directions to the waiting driver. As the car sped away, he glanced in the rearview mirror.

Old Man Gowse stood grimly motionless on the walk in front of Police Headquarters.

"Old Man Cassandra," Chief Underbeck muttered. The driver shot a swift glance at him and stepped on the gas.

Less than two hours after Chief Underbeck arrived back at Wharton's Swamp, the adjacent highway was crowded with cars—state-police patrol cars, cars of the local curious, and Army trucks from Camp Evans.

Promptly at nine o'clock, over three hundred soldiers, police and citizen volunteers, all armed, swung into the swamp to begin a careful search.

Shortly before dusk most of them had arrived at the sea on the far side of the swamp. Their exhaustive efforts had netted nothing. One soldier, noticing fierce eyes glaring out of a tree, had bagged an owl, and one of the state policemen had flushed a young bobcat. Someone else had stepped on a copperhead and been treated for snakebite. But there was no sign of a monster, a murderous tramp, or any of the missing men.

In the face of mounting skepticism, Chief Underbeck stood firm. Pointing out that, so far as they knew to date, the murderer prowled only at night, he ordered that after a four-hour rest and meal period the search should continue.

A number of helicopters which had hovered over the area during the afternoon landed on the strip of shore, bringing food and supplies. At Chief Underbeck's insistence, barriers were set up on the beach. Guards were stationed along the entire length of the highway; powerful searchlights were brought up. Another truck from Camp Evans arrived with a portable machine gun and several flame-throwers.

By eleven o'clock that night, the stage was set. The beach barriers were in place, guards were at station, and huge searchlights, erected near the highway, swept the dismal marsh with probing cones of light.

At eleven-fifteen the night patrols, each consisting of ten strongly armed men, struck into the swamp again.

Ravenous with hunger, the hood of horror reared out of the mud at the bottom of a rancid pool and rose toward the surface. Flopping ashore in the darkness, it slid quickly away over the clumps of scattered swamp grass. It was impelled, as always, by a savage and enormous hunger.

Although hunting in its new environment had been good, its immense appetite knew no appeasement. The more food it consumed, the more it seemed to require.

As it rushed off, alert to the minute vibrations which indicated food, it became aware of various disturbing emanations. Although it was the time of darkness in this strange world, the darkness at this usual hunting period was oddly pierced by the monster's hated enemy—light. The food vibrations were stronger than the shape of slime had ever experienced. They were on all sides, powerful, purposeful, moving in many directions all through the lower layers of puzzling, light-riven darkness.

Lifting out of the ooze, the hood of horror flowed up a lattice-work of gnarled swamp snags and hung motionless, while drops of muddy water rolled off its glistening surface and dripped below. The thing's sensory apparatus told it that the maddening streaks of lack of darkness were everywhere.

Even as it hung suspended on the snags like a great filthy carpet coated with slime, a terrible touch of light slashed through the surrounding darkness and burned against it.

It immediately loosened its hold on the snags and fell back into the ooze with a mighty *plop*. Nearby, the vibrations suddenly increased in intensity. The maddening streamers of light shot through the darkness on all sides.

Baffled and savage, the thing plunged into the ooze and propelled itself in the opposite direction.

But this proved to be only a temporary respite. The vibrations redoubled in intensity. The darkness almost disappeared, riven and pierced by bolts and rivets of light.

For the first time in its incalculable existence, the thing experienced something vaguely akin to fear. The light could not be snatched up and squeezed and smothered to death. It was an alien enemy against which the hood of horror had learned only one defense—flight, hiding.

And now as its world of darkness was torn apart by sudden floods and streamers of light, the monster instinctively sought the refuge afforded by that vast black cradle from which it had climbed.

Flinging itself through the swamp, it headed back for sea.

The guard patrols stationed along the beach, roused by the sound of gunfire and urgent shouts of warning from the interior of the swamp, stood or knelt with ready weapons as the clamor swiftly approached the sea.

The dismal reedy beach lay fully exposed in the harsh glare of searchlights. Waves rolled in toward shore, splashing white crests of foam far up the sands. In the searchlights' illumination the dark waters glistened with an oily iridescence.

The shrill cries increased. The watchers tensed, waiting. And suddenly, across the long dreary flats clotted with weed stalks and sunken drifts, there burst into view a nightmare shape which froze the shore patrols in their tracks.

A thing of slimy blackness, a thing which had no essential shape, no discernible earthly features, rushed through the thorn thickets and onto the flats. It was a shape of utter darkness, one second a great flapping hood, the next a black viscid pool of living ooze which flowed upon itself, sliding forward with incredible speed.

Some of the guards remained rooted where they stood, too overcome with horror to pull the triggers of their weapons. Others broke the spell of terror and began firing. Bullets from half a dozen rifles tore into the black monster speeding across the mud flats.

As the thing neared the end of the flats and approached the first sand dunes of the open beach, the patrol guards who had flushed it from the swamp broke into the open.

One of them paused, bellowing at the beach guards. "It's heading for sea! For God's sake, don't let it escape!"

The beach guards redoubled their firing, suddenly realizing with a kind of sick horror that the monster was apparently unaffected by the rifle slugs. Without a single pause, it rolled through the last fringe of cattails and flopped onto the sands.

As in a hideous nightmare, the guards saw it flap over the nearest sand dune and slide toward the sea. A moment later however, they remembered the barbed-wire beach barrier which Chief Underbeck had stubbornly insisted on their erecting.

Gaining heart, they closed in, running over the dunes toward the spot where the black horror would strike the wire.

Someone in the lead yelled in sudden triumph. "It's caught! It's stuck on the wire!"

The searchlights concentrated swaths of light on the barrier.

The thing had reached the barbed wire fence and apparently flung itself against the twisted strands. Now it appeared to be hopelessly caught; it twisted and flopped and squirmed like some unspeakable giant jellyfish snared in a fisherman's net.

The guards ran forward, sure of their victory. All at once however, the guard in the lead screamed a wild warning. "It's squeezing through! It's getting away!"

In the glare of light they saw with consternation that the monster appeared to be *flowing* through the wire, like a blob of liquescent ooze.

Ahead lay a few yards of downward slanting beach and, beyond that, rolling breakers of the open sea.

There was a collective gasp of horrified dismay as the monster, with a quick forward lurch, squeezed through the barrier. It tilted there briefly, twisting, as if a few last threads of itself might still be entangled in the wire.

As it moved to disengage itself and rush down the wet sands into the black sea, one of the guards hurled himself forward until he was almost abreast of the barrier. Sliding to his knees, he aimed at the escaping hood of horror.

A second later a great searing spout of flame shot from his weapon and burst in a smoky red blossom against the thing on the opposite side of the wire.

Black oily smoke billowed into the night. A ghastly stench flowed over the beach. The guards saw a flaming mass of horror grope away from the barrier. The soldier who aimed the flamethrower held it remorselessly steady.

There was a hideous bubbling, hissing sound. Vast gouts of thick, greasy smoke swirled into the night air. The indescribable stench became almost unbearable.

When the soldier finally shut off the flamethrower, there was nothing in sight except the white-hot glowing wires of the barrier and a big patch of blackened sand.

With good reason the mantle of slime had hated light, for its ultimate source was fire—the final unknown enemy which even the black hood could not drag down and devour.

HOW LOVE CAME TO PROFESSOR GUILDEA

Robert Hichens

DULL PEOPLE OFTEN WONDERED HOW IT CAME ABOUT THAT
Father Murchison and Professor Frederic Guildea were intimate friends. The one was all faith, the other all scepti-
cism. The nature of the Father was based on love. He
viewed the world with an almost childlike tenderness above
his long, black cassock; and his mild, yet perfectly fearless,
blue eyes seemed always to be watching the goodness that
exists in humanity, and rejoicing at what they saw. The
Professor, on the other hand, had a hard face like a hatch-
et, tipped with an aggressive black goatee beard. His eyes
were quick, piercing and irreverent. The lines about his
small, thin-lipped mouth were almost cruel. His voice was
harsh and dry, sometimes, when he grew energetic, almost
soprano. It fired off words with a sharp and clipping utterance. His habitual manner was one of distrust and investigation. It was impossible to suppose that, in his busy life,
he found any time for love, either of humanity in general
or of an individual.

Yet his days were spent in scientific investigations which
conferred immense benefits upon the world.

Both men were celibates. Father Murchison was a member of an Anglican order which forbade him to marry.
Professor Guildea had a poor opinion of most things, but
especially of women. He had formerly held a post as lectur-
er at Birmingham. But when his fame as a discoverer
grew, he removed to London. There, at a lecture he gave in
the East End, he first met Father Murchison. They spoke a
few words. Perhaps the bright intelligence of the priest ap-
pealed to the man of science, who was inclined, as a rule,
to regard the clergy with some contempt. Perhaps the

transparent sincerity of this devotee, full of common sense, attracted him. As he was leaving the hall he abruptly asked the Father to call on him at his house in Hyde Park Place. And the Father, who seldom went into the West End, except to preach, accepted the invitation.

"When will you come?" said Guildea.

He was folding up the blue paper on which his notes were written in a tiny, clear hand. The leaves rustled drily in accompaniment to his sharp, dry voice.

"On Sunday week I am preaching in the evening at St. Savior's, not far off," said the Father.

"I don't go to church."

"No," said the Father, without any accent of surprise or condemnation.

"Come to supper afterwards?"

"Thank you, I will."

"What time will you come?"

The Father smiled.

"As soon as I have finished my sermon. The service is at six-thirty."

"About eight then, I suppose. Don't make the sermon too long. My number in Hyde Park Place is 100. Goodnight to you."

He snapped an elastic band round his papers and strode off without shaking hands.

On the appointed Sunday, Father Murchison preached to a densely crowded congregation at St. Savior's. The subject of his sermon was sympathy, and the comparative uselessness of man in the world unless he can learn to love his neighbour as himself. The sermon was rather long, and when the preacher, in his flowing black cloak, and his hard, round hat, with a straight brim over which hung the ends of a black cord, made his way toward the Professor's house, the hands of the illuminated clock disc at the Marble Arch pointed to twenty minutes past eight.

The Father hurried on, pushing his way through the crowd of standing soldiers, chattering women and giggling street boys in their Sunday best. It was a warm April night, and, when he reached number 100 Hyde Park Place, he found the Professor bareheaded on his doorstep, gazing out toward the Park railings, and enjoying the soft, moist air, in front of his lighted passage.

"Ha, a long sermon!" he exclaimed. "Come in."

"I fear it was," said the Father, obeying the invitation. "I am that dangerous thing—an extempore preacher."

"More attractive to speak without notes, if you can do it. Hang your hat and coat—oh, cloak—here. We'll have supper at once. This is the dining room."

He opened a door on the right and they entered a long, narrow room, with a gold paper and a black ceiling, from which hung an electric lamp with a gold-colored shade. In the room stood a small oval table with covers laid for two. The Professor rang the bell. Then he said:

"People seem to talk better at an oval table than at a square one."

"Really. Is that so?"

"Well, I've had precisely the same party twice, once at a square table, once at an oval table. The first dinner was a dull failure, the second a brilliant success. Sit down, won't you?"

"How d'you account for the difference?" said the Father, sitting down, and pulling the tail of his cassock well under him.

"H'm. I know how you'd account for it."

"Indeed. How then?"

"At an oval table, since there are no corners, the chain of human sympathy—the electric current, is much more complete. Eh! Let me give you some soup."

"Thank you."

The Father took it, and, as he did so, turned his beaming blue eyes on his host. Then he smiled.

"What!" he said, in his pleasant, light tenor voice. "You do go to church sometimes, then?"

"Tonight is the first time for ages. And, mind you, I was tremendously bored."

The Father still smiled, and his blue eyes gently twinkled.

"Dear, dear!" he said, "what a pity!"

"But not by the sermon," Guildea added. "I don't pay a

compliment. I state a fact. The sermon didn't bore me. If it had, I should have said so, or said nothing."

"And which would you have done?"

The Professor smiled almost genially.

"Don't know," he said. "What wine d'you drink?"

"None, thank you. I'm a teetotaller. In my profession and milieu it is necessary to be one. Yes, I will have some soda water. I think you would have done the first."

"Very likely, and very wrongly. You wouldn't have minded much."

"I don't think I should."

They were intimate already. The Father felt most pleasantly at home under the black ceiling. He drank some soda water and seemed to enjoy it more than the Professor enjoyed his claret.

"You smile at the theory of the chain of human sympathy, I see," said the Father. "Then what is your explanation of the failure of your square party with corners, the success of your oval party without them?"

"Probably on the first occasion the wit of the assembly had a chill on his liver, while on the second he was in perfect health. Yet, you see, I stick to the oval table."

"And that means—"

"Very little. By the way, your omission of any allusion to the notorious part liver plays in love was a serious one tonight."

"Your omission of any desire for close human sympathy in your life is a more serious one."

"How can you be sure I have no such desire?"

"I divine it. Your look, your manner, tell me it is so. You were disagreeing with my sermon all the time I was preaching. Weren't you?"

"Part of the time."

The servant changed the plates. He was a middle-aged, blond, thin man, with a stony white face, pale, prominent eyes, and an accomplished manner of service. When he had left the room, the Professor continued.

"Your remarks interested me, but I thought them exaggerated."

"For instance?"

"Let me play the egoist for a moment. I spend most of my time in hard work, very hard work. The results of this work, you will allow, benefit humanity."

"Enormously," assented the Father, thinking of more than one of Guildea's discoveries.

"And the benefit conferred by this work, undertaken merely for its own sake, is just as great as if it were undertaken because I loved my fellowman, and sentimentally desired to see him more comfortable than he is at present. I'm as useful precisely in my present condition of—in my present nonaffectional condition—as I should be if I were as full of gush as the sentimentalists who want to get murderers out of prison, or to put a premium on tyranny—like Tolstoi—by preventing the punishment of tyrants."

"One may do great harm with affection; great good without it. Yes, that is true. Even *le bon motif* is not everything, I know. Still I contend that, given your powers, you would be far more useful in the world with sympathy, affection for your kind, added to them than as you are. I believe even that you would do still more splendid work."

The Professor poured himself out another glass of claret.

"You noticed my butler?" he said.

"I did."

"He's a perfect servant. He makes me perfectly comfortable. Yet he has no feeling of liking for me. I treat him civilly. I pay him well. But I never think about him, or concern myself with him as a human being. I know nothing of his character except what I read of it in his last master's letter. There are, you may say, no truly human relations between us. You would affirm that his work would be better done if I had made him personally like me as man—of any class—can like man—of any other class?"

"I should, decidedly."

"I contend that he couldn't do his work better than he does it at present."

"But if any crisis occurred?"

"What?"

"Any crisis, change in your condition. If you needed his help, not only as a man and a butler, but as a man and a brother? He'd fail you then, probably. You would never get from your servant that finest service which can only be prompted by an honest affection."

"You have finished?"

"Quite."

"Let us go upstairs then. Yes, those are good prints. I picked them up in Birmingham when I was living there. This is my workroom."

They came to a double room lined entirely with books, and brilliantly, rather hardly, lit by electricity. The windows at one end looked on to the Park, at the other on to the garden of a neighboring house. The door by which they entered was concealed from the inner and smaller room by the jutting wall of the outer room, in which stood a huge writing table loaded with letters, pamphlets and manuscripts. Between the two windows of the inner room was a cage in which a large, grey parrot was clambering, using both beak and claws to assist him in his slow and meditative peregrinations.

"You have a pet," said the Father, surprised.

"I possess a parrot," the Professor answered drily, "I got him for a purpose when I was making a study of the imitative powers of birds, and I have never got rid of him. A cigar?"

"Thank you."

They sat down. Father Murchison glanced at the parrot. It had paused in its journey, and, clinging to the bars of its cage, was regarding them with attentive round eyes that looked deliberately intelligent, but by no means sympathetic. He looked away from it to Guildea, who was smoking, with his head thrown back, his sharp, pointed chin, on which the small black beard bristled, upturned. He was moving his under lip up and down rapidly. This action caused the beard to stir and look peculiarly aggressive. The Father suddenly chuckled softly.

"Why's that?" cried Guildea, letting his chin drop down on his breast and looking at his guest sharply.

"I was thinking it would have to be a crisis indeed that

could make you cling to your butler's affection for assistance."

Guildea smiled too.

"You're right. It would. Here he comes."

The man entered with coffee. He offered it gently, and retired like a shadow retreating on a wall.

"Splendid, inhuman fellow," remarked Guildea.

"I prefer the East End lad who does my errands in Bird Street," said the Father. "I know all his worries. He knows some of mine. We are friends. He's more noisy than your man. He even breathes hard when he is especially solicitous, but he would do more for me than put the coals on my fire, or black my square-toed boots."

"Men are differently made. To me the watchful eye of affection would be abominable."

"What about that bird?"

The Father pointed to the parrot. It had got up on its perch and, with one foot uplifted in an impressive, almost benedictory, manner, was gazing steadily at the Professor.

"That's the watchful eye of imitation, with a mind at the back of it, desirous of reproducing the peculiarities of others. No, I thought your sermon tonight very fresh, very clever. But I have no wish for affection. Reasonable liking, of course, one desires"—he tugged sharply at his beard, as if to warn himself against sentimentality—"but anything more would be most irksome, and would push me, I feel sure, toward cruelty. It would also hamper one's work."

"I don't think so."

"The sort of work I do. I shall continue to benefit the world without loving it, and it will continue to accept the benefits without loving me. That's all as it should be."

He drank his coffee. Then he added rather aggressively:

"I have neither time nor inclination for sentimentality."

When Guildea let Father Murchison out, he followed the Father on to the doorstep and stood there for a moment. The Father glanced across the damp road into the Park.

"I see you've got a gate just opposite you," he said idly.

"Yes. I often slip across for a stroll to clear my brain. Good-night to you. Come again some day."

"With pleasure. Good-night."

The priest strode away, leaving Guildea standing on the step.

Father Murchison came many times again to number 100 Hyde Park Place. He had a feeling of liking for most men and women whom he knew, and of tenderness for all, whether he knew them or not, but he grew to have a special sentiment toward Guildea. Strangely enough, it was a sentiment of pity. He pitied this hardworking, eminently successful man of big brain and bold heart, who never seemed depressed, who never wanted assistance, who never complained of the twisted skein of life or faltered in his progress along its way. The Father pitied Guildea, in fact, because Guildea wanted so little. He had told him so, for the intercourse of the two men, from the beginning, had been singularly frank.

One evening, when they were talking together, the Father happened to speak of one of the oddities of life, the fact that those who do not want things often get them, while those who seek them vehemently are disappointed in their search.

"Then I ought to have affection poured upon me," said Guildea smiling rather grimly. "For I hate it."

"Perhaps some day you will."

"I hope not, most sincerely."

Father Murchison said nothing for a moment. He was drawing together the ends of the broad band round his cassock. When he spoke he seemed to be answering someone.

"Yes," he said slowly, "yes, that *is* my feeling—pity."

"For whom?" said the Professor.

Then, suddenly, he understood. He did not say that he understood, but Father Murchison felt, and saw, that it was quite unnecessary to answer his friend's question. So Guildea, strangely enough, found himself closely acquainted with a man—his opposite in all ways—who pitied him.

The fact that he did not mind this, and scarcely ever thought about it, shows perhaps as clearly as anything could, the peculiar indifference of his nature.

II

One Autumn evening, a year and a half after Father
Murchison and the Professor had first met, the Father
called in Hyde Park Place and enquired of the blond and
stony butler—his name was Pitting—whether his master
was at home.

"Yes, sir," replied Pitting. "Will you please come this
way?"

He moved noiselessly up the rather narrow stairs, followed by the Father, tenderly opened the library door, and
in his soft, cold voice, announced:

"Father Murchison."

Guildea was sitting in an armchair, before a small fire.
His thin, long-fingered hands lay outstretched upon his
knees, his head was sunk down on his chest. He appeared
to be pondering deeply. Pitting very slightly raised his
voice.

"Father Murchison to see you, sir," he repeated.

The Professor jumped up rather suddenly and turned
sharply round as the Father came in.

"Oh," he said. "It's you, is it? Glad to see you. Come to
the fire."

The Father glanced at him and thought him looking unusually fatigued.

"You don't look well tonight," the Father said.

"No?"

"You must be working too hard. That lecture you are
going to give in Paris is bothering you?"

"Not a bit. It's all arranged. I could deliver it to you at
this moment verbatim. Well, sit down."

The Father did so, and Guildea sank once more into his
chair and stared hard into the fire without another word.
He seemed to be thinking profoundly. His friend did not
interrupt him, but quietly lit a pipe and began to smoke
reflectively. The eyes of Guildea were fixed upon the fire.
The Father glanced about the room, at the walls of soberly
bound books, at the crowded writing-table, at the windows,
before which hung heavy, dark-blue curtains of old bro-

cade, at the cage, which stood between them. A green baize covering was thrown over it. The Father wondered why. He had never seen Napoleon—so the parrot was named—covered up at night before. While he was looking at the baize, Guildea suddenly jerked up his head, and, taking his hands from his knees and clasping them, said abruptly:

"D'you think I'm an attractive man?"

Father Murchison jumped. Such a question coming from such a man astounded him.

"Bless me!" he ejaculated. "What makes you ask? Do you mean attractive to the opposite sex?"

"That's what I don't know," said the Professor gloomily, and staring again into the fire. "That's what I don't know."

The Father grew more astonished.

"Don't know!" he exclaimed.

And he laid down his pipe.

"Let's say—d'you think I'm attractive, that there's anything about me which might draw a—a human being, or an animal irresistibly to me?"

"Whether you desired it or not?"

"Exactly—or—no, let us say definitely—if I did not desire it."

Father Murchison pursed up his rather full, cherubic lips, and little wrinkles appeared about the corners of his blue eyes.

"There might be, of course," he said, after a pause. "Human nature is weak, engagingly weak, Guildea. And you're inclined to flout it. I could understand a certain class of lady—the lion-hunting, the intellectual lady, seeking you. Your reputation, your great name—"

"Yes, yes," Guildea interrupted, rather irritably—"I know all that, I know."

He twisted his long hands together, bending the palms outwards till his thin, pointed fingers cracked. His forehead was wrinkled in a frown.

"I imagine," he said—he stopped and coughed drily, almost shrilly—"I imagine it would be very disagreeable to be liked, to be run after—that is the usual expression, isn't it—by anything one objected to."

And now he half-turned in his chair, crossed his legs one over the other, and looked at his guest with an unusual, almost piercing interrogation.

"Anything?" said the Father.

"Well—well, anyone. I imagine nothing could be more unpleasant."

"To you—no," answered the Father. "But—forgive me, Guildea, I cannot conceive your permitting such intrusion. You don't encourage adoration."

Guildea nodded his head gloomily.

"I don't," he said, "I don't. That's just it. That's the curious part of it, that I—"

He broke off deliberately, got up and stretched.

"I'll have a pipe, too," he said.

He went over to the mantelpiece, got his pipe, filled it and lighted it. As he held the match to the tobacco, bending forward with an enquiring expression, his eyes fell upon the green baize that covered Napoleon's cage. He threw the match into the grate, and puffed at the pipe as he walked forward to the cage. When he reached it he put out his hand, took hold of the baize and began to pull it away. Then suddenly he pushed it back over the cage.

"No," he said, as if to himself, "no."

He returned rather hastily to the fire and threw himself once more into his armchair.

"You're wondering," he said to Father Murchison. "So am I. I don't know at all what to make of it. I'll just tell you the facts and you must tell me what you think of them. The night before last, after a day of hard work—but no harder than usual—I went to the front door to get a breath of air. You know I often do that."

"Yes, I found you on the doorstep when I first came here."

"Just so. I didn't put on hat or coat. I just stood on the step as I was. My mind, I remember, was still full of my work. It was rather a dark night, not very dark. The hour was about eleven, or a quarter past. I was staring at the Park, and presently I found that my eyes were directed toward somebody who was sitting, back to me, on one of the benches. I saw the person—if it was a person—through the railings."

"If it was a person!" said the Father. "What do you mean by that?"

"Wait a minute. I say that because it was too dark for me to know. I merely saw some blackish object on the bench, rising into view above the level of the back of the seat. I couldn't say it was man, woman or child. But something there was, and I found that I was looking at it."

"I understand."

"Gradually, I also found that my thoughts were becoming fixed upon this thing or person. I began to wonder, first, what it was doing there; next, what it was thinking; lastly, what it was like."

"Some poor creature without a home, I suppose," said the Father.

"I said that to myself. Still, I was taken with an extraordinary interest about this object, so great an interest that I got my hat and crossed the road to go into the Park. As you know, there's an entrance almost opposite to my house. Well, Murchison, I crossed the road, passed through the gate in the railings, went up to the seat, and found that there was—nothing on it."

"Were you looking at it as you walked?"

"Part of the time. But I removed my eyes from it just as I passed through the gate, because there was a row going on a little way off, and I turned for an instant in that direction. When I saw that the seat was vacant, I was seized by a most absurd sensation of disappointment, almost of anger. I stopped and looked about me to see if anything was moving away, but I could see nothing. It was a cold night and misty, and there were few people about. Feeling, as I say, foolishly and unnaturally disappointed, I retraced my steps to this house. When I got here, I discovered that during my short absence I had left the hall door open—half open."

"Rather imprudent in London."

"Yes. I had no idea, of course, that I had done so, till I got back. However, I was only away three minutes or so."

"Yes."

"It was not likely that anybody had gone in."

"I suppose not."

"Was it?"

"Why do you ask me that, Guildea?"

"Well, well!"

"Besides, if anybody had gone in, on your return you'd have caught him, surely."

Guildea coughed again. The Father, surprised, could not fail to recognize that he was nervous and that his nervousness was affecting him physically.

"I must have caught cold that night," he said, as if he had read his friend's thought and hastened to contradict it. Then he went on:

"I entered the hall, or passage, rather."

He paused again. His uneasiness was becoming very apparent.

"And you did catch somebody?" said the Father.

Guildea cleared his throat.

"That's just it," he said, "now we come to it. I'm not imaginative, as you know."

"You certainly are not."

"No, but hardly had I stepped into the passage before I felt certain that somebody had got into the house during my absence. I felt convinced of it, and not only that, I also felt convinced that the intruder was the very person I had dimly seen sitting upon the seat in the Park. What d'you say to that?"

"I begin to think you are imaginative."

"H'm! It seemed to me that the person—the occupant of the seat—and I, had simultaneously formed the project of interviewing each other, had simultaneously set out to put that project into execution. I became so certain of this that I walked hastily upstairs into this room, expecting to find the visitor awaiting me. But there was no one. I then came down again and went into the dining room. No one. I was actually astonished. Isn't that odd?"

"Very," said the Father, quite gravely.

The Professor's chill and gloomy manner, and uncomfortable, constrained appearance kept away the humor that might well have lurked round the steps of such a discourse.

"I went upstairs again," he continued, "sat down and thought the matter over. I resolved to forget it, and took up a book. I might perhaps have been able to read, but suddenly I thought I noticed—"

He stopped abruptly. Father Murchison observed that he was staring towards the green baize that covered the parrot's cage.

"But that's nothing," he said. "Enough that I couldn't read. I resolved to explore the house. You know how small it is, how easily one can go all over it. I went all over it. I went into every room without exception. To the servants, who were having supper, I made some excuse. They were surprised at my advent, no doubt."

"And Pitting?"

"Oh, he got up politely when I came in, stood while I was there, but never said a word. I muttered 'don't disturb yourselves,' or something of the sort, and came out. Murchison, I found nobody new in the house—yet I returned to this room entirely convinced that somebody had entered while I was in the Park."

"And gone out again before you came back?"

"No, had stayed, and was still in the house."

"But, my dear Guildea," began the Father, now in great astonishment. "Surely—"

"I know what you want to say—what I should want to say in your place. Now, do wait. I am also convinced that this visitor has not left the house and is at this moment in it."

He spoke with evident sincerity, with extreme gravity. Father Murchison looked him full in the face, and met his quick, keen eyes.

"No," he said, as if in reply to an uttered question: "I'm perfectly sane. I assure you. The whole matter seems almost as incredible to me as it must to you. But, as you know, I never quarrel with facts, however strange. I merely try to examine into them thoroughly. I have already consulted a doctor and been pronounced in perfect bodily health."

He paused, as if expecting the Father to say something.

"Go on, Guildea," he said, "you haven't finished."

"No. I felt that night positive that somebody had entered the house, and remained in it, and my conviction grew. I went to bed as usual, and, contrary to my expectation, slept as well as I generally do. Yet directly I woke up yesterday morning I knew that my household had been increased by one."

"May I interrupt you for one moment? How did you know it?"

"By my mental sensation. I can only say that I was perfectly conscious of a new presence within my house, close to me."

"How very strange," said the Father. "And you feel absolutely certain that you are not overworked? Your brain does not feel tired? Your head is quite clear?"

"Quite. I was never better. When I came down to breakfast that morning I looked sharply into Pitting's face. He was as coldly placid and inexpressive as usual. It was evident to me that his mind was in no way distressed. After breakfast I sat down to work, all the time ceaselessly conscious of the fact of this intruder upon my privacy. Nevertheless, I labored for several hours, waiting for any development that might occur to clear away the mysterious obscurity of this event. I lunched. About half-past two I was obliged to go out to attend a lecture. I therefore took my coat and hat, opened my door, and stepped onto the pavement. I was instantly aware that I was no longer intruded upon, and this although I was now in the street, surrounded by people. Consequently, I felt certain that the thing in my house must be thinking of me, perhaps even spying upon me."

"Wait a moment," interrupted the Father. "What was your sensation? Was it one of fear?"

"Oh, dear no. I was entirely puzzled—as I am now—and keenly interested, but not in any way alarmed. I delivered my lecture with my usual ease and returned home in the evening. On entering the house again I was perfectly conscious that the intruder was still there. Last night I dined alone and spent the hours after dinner in reading a scientific work in which I was deeply interested. While I read, however, I never for one moment lost the knowledge that some mind—very attentive to me—was within hail of mine. I will say more than this—the sensation constantly increased, and, by the time I got up to go to bed, I had come to a very strange conclusion."

"What? What was it?"

"That whoever—or whatever—had entered my house during my short absence in the Park was more than interested in me."

"More than interested in you?"

"Was fond, or was becoming fond, of me."

"Oh!" exclaimed the Father. "Now I understand why you asked me just now whether I thought there was anything about you that might draw a human being or an animal irresistibly to you."

"Precisely. Since I came to this conclusion, Murchison, I will confess that my feeling of strong curiosity has become tinged with another feeling."

"Of fear?"

"No, of dislike, or irritation. No—not fear, not fear."

As Guildea repeated unnecessarily this asseveration, he looked again toward the parrot's cage.

"What is there to be afraid of in such a matter?" he added. "I am not a child to tremble before bogies."

In saying the last words he raised his voice sharply; then he walked quickly to the cage, and, with an abrupt movement, pulled the baize covering from it. Napoleon was disclosed, apparently dozing upon his perch with his head held slightly on one side. As the light reached him, he moved, ruffled the feathers about his neck, blinked his eyes, and began slowly to sidle to and fro, thrusting his head forward and drawing it back with an air of complacent, though rather unmeaning, energy. Guildea stood by the cage, looking at him closely, and indeed with an attention that was so intense as to be remarkable, almost unnatural.

"How absurd these birds are!" he said at length, coming back to the fire.

"You have no more to tell me?" asked the Father.

"No. I am still aware of the presence of something in

my house. I am still conscious of its close attention to me. I am still irritated, seriously annoyed—I confess it—by that attention."

"You say you are aware of the presence of something at this moment?"

"At this moment—yes."

"Do you mean in this room, with us, now?"

"I should say so—at any rate, quite near us."

Again he glanced quickly, almost suspiciously, toward the cage of the parrot. The bird was sitting still on its perch now. Its head was bent down and cocked sideways, and it appeared to be listening attentively to something.

"That bird will have the intonations of my voice more correctly than ever by tomorrow morning," said the Father, watching Guildea closely with his mild blue eyes. "And it has always imitated me very cleverly."

The Professor started slightly.

"Yes," he said. "Yes, no doubt. Well, what do you make of this affair?"

"Nothing at all. It is absolutely inexplicable. I can speak quite frankly to you, I feel sure."

"Of course. That's why I have told you the whole thing."

"I think you must be overworked, overstrained, without knowing it."

"And that the doctor was mistaken when he said I was all right?"

"Yes."

Guildea knocked his pipe out against the chimney piece.

"It may be so," he said, "I will not be so unreasonable as to deny the possibility, although I feel as well as I ever did in my life. What do you advise then?"

"A week of complete rest away from London, in good air."

"The usual prescription. I'll take it. I'll go tomorrow to Westgate and leave Napoleon to keep house in my absence."

For some reason, which he could not explain to himself, the pleasure which Father Murchison felt in hearing the first part of his friend's final remark was lessened, was almost destroyed, by the last sentence.

He walked toward the City that night, deep in thought, remembering and carefully considering the first interview he had with Guildea in the latter's house a year and a half before.

On the following morning Guildea left London.

III

Father Murchison was so busy a man that he had little time for brooding over the affairs of others. During Guildea's week at the sea, however, the Father thought about him a great deal, with much wonder and some dismay. The dismay was soon banished, for the mild-eyed priest was quick to discern weakness in himself, quicker still to drive it forth as a most undesirable inmate of the soul. But the wonder remained. It was destined to a crescendo. Guildea had left London on a Thursday. On a Thursday he returned, having previously sent a note to Father Murchison to mention that he was leaving Westgate at a certain time. When his train ran into Victoria Station, at five o'cock in the evening, he was surprised to see the cloaked figure of his friend standing upon the grey platform behind a line of porters.

"What, Murchison!" he said. "You here! Have you seceded from your order that you are taking this holiday?"

They shook hands.

"No," said the Father. "It happened that I had to be in this neighborhood today, visiting a sick person. So I thought I would meet you."

"And see if I were still a sick person, eh?"

The professor glanced at him kindly, but with a dry little laugh.

"Are you?" replied the Father gently, looking at him with interest. "No, I think not. You appear very well."

The sea air had, in fact, put some brownish red into Guildea's always thin cheeks. His keen eyes were shining with life and energy, and he walked forward in his loose grey suit and fluttering overcoat with a vigor that was noticeable, carrying easily in his left hand his well-filled Gladstone bag.

The Father felt completely reassured.

"I never saw you look better," he said.

"I never was better. Have you an hour to spare?"

"Two."

"Good. I'll send my bag up by cab, and we'll walk across the Park to my house and have a cup of tea there. What d'you say?"

"I shall enjoy it."

They walked out of the station yard, past the flower girls and newspaper sellers towards Grosvenor Place.

"And you have had a pleasant time?" the Father said.

"Pleasant enough, and lonely. I left my companion behind me in the passage at number 100, you know."

"And you'll not find him there now, I feel sure."

"H'm!" ejaculated Guildea. "What a precious weakling you think me, Murchison."

As he spoke he strode forward more quickly, as if moved to emphasize his sensation of bodily vigor.

"A weakling—no. But anyone who uses his brain as persistently as you do yours must require an occasional holiday."

"And I required one very badly, eh?"

"You required one, I believe."

"Well, I've had it. And now we'll see."

The evening was closing in rapidly. They crossed the road at Hyde Park Corner, and entered the Park, in which were a number of people going home from work; men in corduroy trousers, caked with dried mud, and carrying tin cans slung over their shoulders, and flat panniers, in which lay their tools. Some of the younger ones talked loudly or whistled shrilly as they walked.

"Until the evening," murmured Father Murchison to himself.

"What?" asked Guildea.

"I was only quoting the last words of the text, which seems written upon life, especially upon the life of pleasure: 'Man goeth forth to his work, and to his labor.' "

"Ah, those fellows are not half-bad fellows to have in an audience. There were a lot of them at the lecture I gave when I first met you, I remember. One of them tried to heckle me. He had a red beard. Chaps with red beards are always hecklers. I laid him low on that occasion. Well, Murchison, and now we're going to see."

"What?"

"Whether my companion has departed."

"Tell me—do you feel any expectation of—well—of again thinking something is there?"

"How carefully you choose language. No, I merely wonder."

"You have no apprehension?"

"Not a scrap. But I confess to feeling curious."

"Then the sea air hasn't taught you to recognize that the whole thing came from overstrain."

"No," said Guildea, very drily.

He walked on in silence for a minute. Then he added:

"You thought it would?"

"I certainly thought it might."

"Make me realize that I had a sickly, morbid, rotten imagination—eh? Come now, Murchison, why not say frankly that you packed me off to Westgate to get rid of what you considered an acute form of hysteria?"

The Father was quite unmoved by this attack.

"Come now, Guildea," he retorted, "what did you expect me to think? I saw no indication of hysteria in you. I never have. One would suppose you the last man likely to have such a malady. But which is more natural—for me to believe in your hysteria or in the truth of such a story as you told me?"

"You have me there. No, I mustn't complain. Well, there's no hysteria about me now, at any rate."

"And no stranger in your house, I hope."

Father Murchison spoke the last words with earnest gravity, dropping the half-bantering tone—which they had both assumed.

"You take the matter very seriously, I believe," said Guildea, also speaking more gravely.

"How else can I take it? You wouldn't have me laugh at it when you tell it me seriously?"

"No. If we find my visitor still in the house, I may even call upon you to exorcise it. But first I must do one thing."

"And that is?"

"Prove to you, as well as to myself, that it is still there."

"That might be difficult," said the Father, considerably surprised by Guildea's matter-of-fact tone.

"I don't know. If it has remained in my house I think I can find a means. And I shall not be at all surprised if it is still there—despite the Westgate air."

In saying the last words the Professor relapsed into his former tone of dry chaff. The Father could not quite make up his mind whether Guildea was feeling unusually grave or unusually gay. As the two men drew near to Hyde Park Place their conversation died away and they walked forward silently in the gathering darkness.

"Here we are!" said Guildea at last.

He thrust his key into the door, opened it and let Father Murchison into the passage, following him closely, and banging the door.

"Here we are!" he repeated in a louder voice.

The electric light was turned on in anticipation of his arrival. He stood still and looked round.

"We'll have some tea at once," he said. "Ah, Pitting!"

The pale butler, who had heard the door bang, moved gently forward from the top of the stairs that led to the kitchen, greeted his master respectfully, took his coat and Father Murchison's cloak, and hung them on two pegs against the wall.

"All's right, Pitting? All's as usual?" said Guildea.

"Quite so, sir."

"Bring us up some tea to the library."

"Yes, sir."

Pitting retreated. Guildea waited till he had disappeared, then opened the dining-room door, put his head into the room and kept it there for a moment, standing perfectly still. Presently he drew back into the passage, shut the door, and said:

"Let's go upstairs."

Father Murchison looked at him enquiringly, but made no remark. They ascended the stairs and came into the library. Guildea glanced rather sharply round. A fire was burning on the hearth. The blue curtains were drawn. The bright gleam of the strong electric light fell on the long rows of books, on the writing table—very orderly in consequence of Guildea's holiday—and on the uncovered cage of the parrot. Guildea went up to the cage. Napoleon was sitting humped up on his perch with his feathers ruffled. His long toes, which looked as if they were covered with crocodile skin, clung to the bar. His round and blinking eyes were filmy, like old eyes. Guildea stared at the bird very hard, and then clucked with his tongue against his teeth. Napoleon shook himself, lifted one foot, extended his toes, sidled along the perch to the bars nearest to the Professor and thrust his head against them. Guildea scratched it with his forefinger two or three times, still gazing attentively at the parrot; then he returned to the fire just as Pitting entered with the tea-tray.

Father Murchison was already sitting in an armchair on one side of the fire. Guildea took another chair and began to pour out tea, as Pitting left the room, closing the door gently behind him. The Father sipped his tea, found it hot and set the cup down on a little table at his side.

"You're fond of that parrot, aren't you?" he asked his friend.

"Not particularly. It's interesting to study sometimes. The parrot mind and nature are peculiar."

"How long have you had him?"

"About four years. I nearly got rid of him just before I made your acquaintance. I'm very glad now I kept him."

"Are you? Why is that?"

"I shall probably tell you in a day or two."

The Father took his cup again. He did not press Guildea for an immediate explanation, but when they had both finished their tea he said:

"Well, has the sea air had the desired effect?"

"No," said Guildea.

The Father brushed some crumbs from the front of his cassock and sat up higher in his chair.

"Your visitor is still here?" he asked, and his blue eyes became almost ungentle and piercing as he gazed at his friend.

"Yes," answered Guildea, calmly.

"How do you know it, when did you know it—when you looked into the dining room just now?"

"No. Not until I came into this room. It welcomed me here."

"Welcomed you! In what way?"

"Simply by being here, by making me feel that it is here, as I might feel that a man was if I came into the room when it was dark."

He spoke quietly, with perfect composure in his usual dry manner.

"Very well," the Father said, "I shall not try to contend against your sensation, or to explain it away. Naturally, I am in amazement."

"So am I. Never has anything in my life surprised me so much. Murchison, of course I cannot expect you to believe more than that I honestly—imagine, if you like—that there is some intruder here, of what kind I am totally unaware. I cannot expect you to believe that there really is anything. If you were in my place, I in yours, I should certainly consider you the victim of some nervous delusion. I could not do otherwise. But—wait. Don't condemn me as a hysteria patient, or as a madman, for two or three days. I feel convinced that—unless I am indeed unwell, a mental invalid, which I don't think is possible—I shall be able very shortly to give you some proof that there is a newcomer in my house."

"You don't tell me what kind of proof?"

"Not yet. Things must go a little farther first. But, perhaps even tomorrow I may be able to explain myself more fully. In the meanwhile, I'll say this, that if, eventually, I can't bring any kind of proof that I'm not dreaming, I'll let you take me to any doctor you like, and I'll resolutely try to adopt your present view—that I'm suffering from an absurd delusion. That is your view, of course?'"

Father Murchison was silent for a moment. Then he said, rather doubtfully:

"It ought to be."

"But isn't it?" asked Guildea, surprised.

"Well, you know, your manner is enormously convincing. Still, of course, I doubt. How can I do otherwise? The whole thing must be fancy."

The Father spoke as if he were trying to recoil from a mental position he was being forced to take up.

"It must be fancy," he repeated.

"I'll convince you by more than my manner, or I'll not try to convince you at all," said Guildea.

When they parted that evening, he said:

"I'll write to you in a day or two probably. I think the proof I am going to give you has been accumulating during my absence. But I shall soon know."

Father Murchison was extremely puzzled as he sat on the top of the omnibus going homeward.

IV

In two days' time he received a note from Guildea asking him to call, if possible, the same evening. This he was unable to do as he had an engagement to fulfil at some East End gathering. The following day was Sunday. He wrote saying he would come on the Monday, and got a wire shortly afterwards: "Yes, Monday come to dinner seven-thirty. Guildea." At half-past seven he stood on the doorstep of number 100.

Pitting let him in.

"Is the Professor quite well, Pitting?" the Father enquired as he took off his cloak.

"I believe so, sir. He has not made any complaint," the butler formally replied. "Will you come upstairs, sir?"

Guildea met them at the door of the library. He was very pale and somber, and shook hands carelessly with his friend.

"Give us dinner," he said to Pitting.

As the butler retired, Guildea shut the door rather cautiously. Father Murchison had never before seen him look so disturbed.

"You're worried, Guildea," the Father said. "Seriously worried."

"Yes, I am. This business is beginning to tell on me a good deal."

"Your belief in the presence of something here continues, then?"

"Oh, dear, yes. There's no sort of doubt about the matter. The night I went across the road into the Park something got into the house, though what the devil it is I can't yet find out. But now, before we go down to dinner, I'll just tell you something about that proof I promised you. You remember?"

"Naturally."

"Can't you imagine what it might be?"

Father Murchison moved his head to express a negative reply.

"Look about the room," said Guildea. "What do you see?"

The Father glanced around the room, slowly and carefully.

"Nothing unusual. You do not mean to tell me there is any appearance of—"

"Oh, no, no, there's no conventional, white-robed, cloud-like figure. Bless my soul, no! I haven't fallen so low as that."

He spoke with considerable irritation.

"Look again."

Father Murchison looked at him, turned in the direction of his fixed eyes and saw the grey parrot clambering in its cage, slowly and persistently.

"What?" he said, quickly. "Will the proof come from there?"

The Professor nodded.

"I believe so," he said. "Now let's go down to dinner. I want some food badly."

They descended to the dining room. While they ate and Pitting waited upon them, the Professor talked about birds, their habits, their curiosities, their fears and their powers of imitation. He had evidently studied this subject with the thoroughness that was characteristic of him in all that he did.

"Parrots," he said presently, "are extraordinarily observant. It is a pity that their means of reproducing what they see are so limited. If it were not so, I have little doubt that their echo of gesture would be as remarkable as their echo of voice often is."

"But hands are missing."

"Yes. They do many things with their heads, however. I once knew an old woman near Goring on the Thames. She was afflicted with the palsy. She held her head perpetually sideways and it trembled, moving from right to left. Her sailor son brought her home a parrot from one of his voyages. It used to reproduce the old woman's palsied movement of the head exactly. Those grey parrots are always on the watch."

Guildea said the last sentence slowly and deliberately, glancing sharply over his wine at Father Murchison, and, when he had spoken it, a sudden light of comprehension dawned in the Priest's mind. He opened his lips to make a swift remark. Guildea turned his bright eyes toward Pitting, who at the moment was tenderly bearing a cheese meringue from the lift that connected the dining room with the lower regions. The Father closed his lips again. But presently, when the butler had placed some apples on the table, had meticulously arranged the decanters, brushed away the crumbs and evaporated, he said, quickly:

"I begin to understand. You think Napoleon is aware of the intruder?"

"I know it. He has been watching my visitant ever since the night of that visitant's arrival."

Another flash of light came to the Priest.

"That was why you covered him with green baize one evening?"

"Exactly. An act of cowardice. His behavior was beginning to grate upon my nerves."

Guildea pursed up his thin lips and drew his brows down, giving to his face a look of sudden pain.

"But now I intend to follow his investigations," he add-

ed, straightening his features. "The week I wasted at Westgate was not wasted by him in London, I can assure you.
Have an apple."

"No, thank you; no, thank you."

The Father repeated the words without knowing that he
did so. Guildea pushed away his glass.

"Let us come upstairs, then."

"No, thank you," reiterated the Father.

"Eh?"

"What am I saying?" exclaimed the Father, getting up.
"I was thinking over this extraordinary affair."

"Ah, you're beginning to forget the hysteria theory?"

They walked out into the passage.

"Well, you are so very practical about the whole matter."

"Why not? Here's something very strange and abnormal
come into my life. What should I do but investigate it
closely and calmly?"

"What, indeed?"

The Father began to feel rather bewildered, under a sort
of compulsion which seemed laid upon him to give earnest
attention to a matter that ought to strike him—so he felt—
as entirely absurd. When they came into the library his
eyes immediately turned, with profound curiosity, toward
the parrot's cage. A slight smile curled the Professor's lips.
He recognized the effect he was producing upon his friend.
The Father saw the smile.

"Oh, I'm not won over yet," he said in answer to it.

"I know. Perhaps you may be before the evening is over.
Here comes the coffee. After we have drunk it, we'll
proceed to our experiment. Leave the coffee, Pitting, and
don't disturb us again."

"No, sir."

"I won't have it black tonight," said the Father, "plenty
of milk, please. I don't want my nerves played upon."

"Suppose we don't take coffee at all?" said Guildea. "If
we do, you may trot out the theory that we are not in a perfectly normal condition. I know you, Murchison, devout
Priest and devout sceptic."

The Father laughed and pushed away his cup.

"Very well, then. No coffee."

"One cigarette, and then to business."

The grey blue smoke curled up.

"What are we going to do?" said the Father.

He was sitting bolt upright as if ready for action. Indeed there was no suggestion of repose in the attitudes of either of the men.

"Hide ourselves, and watch Napoleon. By the way—that reminds me."

He got up, went to a corner of the room, picked up a piece of green baize and threw it over the cage.

"I'll pull that off when we are hidden."

"And tell me first if you have had any manifestation of this supposed presence during the last few days?"

"Merely an increasingly intense sensation of something here, perpetually watching me, perpetually attending to all my doings."

"Do you feel that it follows you about?"

"Not always. It was in this room when you arrived. It is here now—I feel. But, in going down to dinner, we seemed to get away from it. The conclusion is that it remained here. Don't let us talk about it just now."

They spoke of other things till their cigarettes were finished. Then, as they threw away the smoldering ends, Guildea said:

"Now, Murchison, for the sake of this experiment, I suggest that we should conceal ourselves behind the curtains on either side of the cage, so that the bird's attention may not be drawn toward us and so distracted from that which we want to know more about. I will pull away the green baize when we are hidden. Keep perfectly still, watch the bird's proceedings, and tell me afterwards how you feel about them, how you explain them. Tread softly."

The Father obeyed, and they stole toward the curtains that fell before the two windows. The Father concealed himself behind those on the left of the cage, the Professor behind those on the right. The latter, as soon as they were hidden, stretched out his arm, drew the baize down from the cage, and let it fall on the floor.

The parrot, which had evidently fallen asleep in the warm darkness, moved on its perch as the light shone upon

it, ruffled the feathers round its throat, and lifted first one
foot and then the other. It turned its head round on its sup-
ple, and apparently elastic, neck, and, diving its beak into
the down upon its back, made some searching investigations with, as it seemed, a satisfactory result, for it soon
lifted its head again, glanced around its cage, and began to
address itself to a nut which had been fixed between the
bars for its refreshment. With its curved beak it felt and
tapped the nut, at first gently, then with severity. Finally
it plucked the nut from the bars, seized it with its rough
grey toes, and, holding it down firmly on the perch,
cracked it and pecked out its contents, scattering some
on the floor of the cage and letting the fractured shell
fall into the china bath that was fixed against the bars. This
accomplished, the bird paused meditatively, extended one
leg backwards, and went through an elaborate process of
wing-stretching that made it look as if it were lopsided and
deformed. With its head reversed, it again applied itself to
a subtle and exhaustive search among the feathers of its
wing. This time its investigation seemed interminable, and
Father Murchison had time to realize the absurdity of the
whole position, and to wonder why he had lent himself to
it. Yet he did not find his sense of humor laughing at it. On
the contrary, he was smitten by a sudden gust of horror.
When he was talking to his friend and watching him, the
Professor's manner, generally so calm, even so prosaic,
vouched for the truth of his story and the well-adjusted
balance of his mind. But when he was hidden this was not
so. And Father Murchison, standing behind his curtain,
with his blue eyes upon the unconcerned Napoleon, began
to whisper to himself the word—madness, with a quicken-
ing sensation of pity and of dread.

The parrot sharply contracted one wing, ruffled the
feathers around its throat again, then extended its other leg
backwards, and proceeded to the cleaning of its other
wing. In the still room the dry sound of the feathers being
spread was distinctly audible. Father Murchison saw the
blue curtains behind which Guildea stood tremble slightly,
as if a breath of wind had come through the window they
shrouded. The clock in the far room chimed, and a coal

dropped into the grate, making a noise like dead leaves
stirring abruptly on hard ground. And again a gust of pity
and of dread swept over the Father. It seemed to him that
he had behaved very foolishly, if not wrongly, in encour-
aging what must surely be the strange dementia of his
friend. He ought to have declined to lend himself to a
proceeding that, ludicrous, even childish in itself, might
well be dangerous in the encouragement it gave to a dis-
eased expectation. Napoleon's protruding leg, extended
wing and twisted neck, his busy and unconscious devotion
to the arrangement of his person, his evident sensation of
complete loneliness, most comfortable solitude, brought
home with vehemence to the Father the undignified
buffoonery of his conduct; the more piteous buffoonery of
his friend. He seized the curtains with his hand and was
about to thrust them aside and issue forth, when an abrupt
movement of the parrot stopped him. The bird, as if
sharply attracted by something, paused in its pecking, and,
with its head still bent backward and twisted sideways on
its neck, seemed to listen intently. Its round eye looked
glistening and strained, like the eye of a disturbed pigeon.
Contracting its wing, it lifted its head and sat for a moment
erect on its perch, shifting its feet mechanically up and
down, as if a dawning excitement produced in it an uncon-
trollable desire of movement. Then it thrust its head forward in the direction of the farther room and remained
perfectly still. Its attitude so strongly suggested the concen-
tration of its attention on something immediately before it,
that Father Murchison instinctively stared about the room,
half-expecting to see Pitting advance softly, having entered
through the hidden door. He did not come, and there was
no sound in the chamber. Nevertheless, the parrot was obviously getting excited and increasingly attentive. It bent its
head lower and lower, stretching out its neck until, almost
falling from the perch, it half-extended its wings, raising
them slightly from its back, as if about to take flight, and
fluttering them rapidly up and down. It continued this fluttering movement for what seemed to the Father an immense time. At length, raising its wings as far as possible,
it dropped them slowly and deliberately down to its back,

caught hold of the edge of its bath with its beak, hoisted itself onto the floor of the cage, waddled to the bars, thrust its head against them, and stood quite still in the exact attitude it always assumed when its head was being scratched by the Professor. So complete was the suggestion of this delight conveyed by the bird, that Father Murchison felt as if he saw a white finger gently pushed among the soft feathers of its head, and he was seized by a most strong conviction that something, unseen by him but seen and welcomed by Napoleon, stood immediately before the cage.

The parrot presently withdrew its head, as if the coaxing finger, had been lifted from it, and its pronounced air of acute physical enjoyment faded into one of marked attention and alert curiosity. Pulling itself up by the bars it climbed again upon its perch, sidled to the left side of the cage, and began apparently to watch something with profound interest. It bowed its head oddly, paused for a moment, then bowed its head again. Father Murchison found himself conceiving—from this elaborate movement of the head—a distinct idea of a personality. The bird's proceedings suggested extreme sentimentality combined with that sort of weak determination which is often the most persistent. Such weak determination is a very common attribute of persons who are partially idiotic. Father Murchison was moved to think of these poor creatures who will often, so strangely and unreasonable, attach themselves with persistence to those who love them least. Like many priests, he had had some experience of them, for the amorous idiot is peculiarly sensitive to the attraction of preachers. This bowing movement of the parrot recalled to his memory a terrible, pale woman who for a time haunted all churches in which he ministered, who was perpetually endeavoring to catch his eye, and who always bent her head with an obsequious and cunningly conscious smile when she did so. The parrot went on bowing, making a short pause between each genuflection, as if it waited for a signal to be given that called into play its imitative faculty.

"Yes, yes, it's imitating an idiot," Father Murchison caught himself saying as he watched.

And he looked again about the room, but saw nothing; except the furniture, the dancing fire, and the serried ranks of the books. Presently the parrot ceased from bowing, and assumed the concentrated and stretched attitude of one listening very keenly. He opened his beak, showing his black tongue, shut it, then opened it again. The Father thought he was going to speak, but he remained silent, although it was obvious that he was trying to bring out something. He bowed again two or three times, paused, and then, again opening his beak, made some remark. The Father could not distinguish any words, but the voice was sickly and disagreeable, a cooing and, at the same time, querulous voice, like a woman's, he thought. And he put his ear nearer to the curtain, listening with almost feverish attention. The bowing was resumed, but this time Napoleon added to it a sidling movement, affectionate and affected, like the movement of a silly and eager thing, nestling up to someone, or giving someone a gentle and furtive nudge. Again the Father thought of that terrible, pale woman who had haunted churches. Several times he had come upon her waiting for him after evening services. Once she had hung her head smiling, and lolled out her tongue and pushed against him sideways in the dark. He remembered how his flesh had shrunk from the poor thing, the sick loathing of her that he could not banish by remembering that her mind was all astray. The parrot paused, listened, opening his beak, and again said something in the same dovelike, amorous voice, full of sickly suggestion and yet hard, even dangerous, in its intonation. A loathsome voice, the Father thought it. But this time, although he heard the voice more distinctly than before, he could not make up his mind whether it was like a woman's voice or a man's—or perhaps a child's. It seemed to be a human voice, and yet oddly sexless. In order to resolve his doubt he withdrew into the darkness of the curtains, ceased to watch Napoleon and simply listened with keen attention, striving to forget that he was listening to a bird, and to imagine that he was overhearing a human being in conversation. After two or three minutes' silence the voice spoke again, and at some length, apparently repeating several times an affec-

tionate series of ejaculations with a cooing emphasis that
was unutterably mawkish and offensive. The sickliness of
the voice, its falling intonations and its strange indelicacy,
combined with a die-away softness and meretricious refine-
ment, made the Father's flesh creep. Yet he could not distinguish any words, nor could he decide on the voice's
sex or age. One thing alone he was certain of as he stood
still in the darkness—that such a sound could only proceed from something peculiarly loathsome, could only
express a personality unendurably abominable to him,
if not to everybody. The voice presently failed, in a sort of
husky gasp, and there was a prolonged silence. It was broken by the Professor, who suddenly pulled away the curtains that hid the Father and said to him:

"Come out now, and look."

The Father came into the light, blinking, glanced toward
the cage, and saw Napoleon poised motionless on one foot
with his head under his wing. He appeared to be asleep.
The Professor was pale, and his mobile lips were drawn
into an expression of supreme disgust.

"Faugh!" he said.

He walked to the windows of the farther room, pulled
aside the curtains and pushed the glass up, letting in the
air. The bare trees were visible in the gray gloom outside.
Guildea leaned out for a minute drawing the night air into
his lungs. Presently he turned round to the Father, and exclaimed abruptly:

"Pestilent! Isn't it?"

"Yes—most pestilent."

"Ever hear anything like it?"

"Not exactly."

"Nor I. It gives me nausea, Murchison, absolute physical
nausea."

He closed the window and walked uneasily about the
room.

"What d'you make of it?" he asked, over his shoulder.

"How d'you mean exactly?"

"Is it man's, woman's, or child's voice?"

"I can't tell, I can't make up my mind."

"Nor I."

"Have you heard it often?"

"Yes, since I returned from Westgate. There are never any words that I can distinguish. What a voice!"

He spat into the fire.

"Forgive me," he said, throwing himself down in a chair. "It turns my stomach—literally."

"And mine," said the Father truly.

"The worst of it is," continued Guildea, with a high, nervous accent, "that there's no brain with it, none at all—only the cunning of idiocy."

The Father started at this exact expression of his own conviction by another.

"Why d'you start like that?" said Guildea, with a quick suspicion which showed the unnatural condition of his nerves.

"Well, the very same idea had occurred to me."

"What?"

"That I was listening to the voice of something idiotic."

"Ah! That's the devil of it, you know, to a man like me. I could fight against brain—but this!"

He sprang up again, poked the fire violently, then stood on the hearth rug with his back to it, and his hands thrust into the high pockets of his trousers.

"That's the voice of the thing that's got into my house," he said. "Pleasant, isn't it?"

And now there was really horror in his eyes, and his voice.

"I must get it out," he exclaimed. "I must get it out. But how?"

He tugged at his short black beard with a quivering hand.

"How?" he continued. "For what is it? Where is it?"

"You feel it's here—now?"

"Undoubtedly. But I couldn't tell you in what part of the room."

He stared about, glancing rapidly at everything.

"Then you consider yourself haunted?" said Father Murchison. He, too, was much moved and disturbed, although he was not conscious of the presence of anything near them in the room.

"I have never believed in any nonsense of that kind, as
you know," Guildea answered. "I simply state a fact,
which I cannot understand, and which is beginning to be
very painful to me. There is something here. But whereas
most so-called hauntings have been described to me as inimical, what I am conscious of is that I am admired, loved,
desired. This is distinctly horrible to me, Murchison, distinctly horrible."

Father Murchison suddenly remembered the first evening
he had spent with Guildea, and the latter's expression
almost of disgust, at the idea of receiving warm affection from anyone. In the light of that long-ago conversation, the present event seemed supremely strange, and almost like a punishment for an offence committed by the
Professor against humanity. But, looking up at his friend's
twitching face, the Father resolved not to be caught in the
net of his hideous belief.

"There can be nothing here," he said. "It's impossible."

"What does the bird imitate, then?"

"The voice of someone who has been here."

"Within the last week then. For it never spoke like that
before, and mind, I noticed that it was watching and striving to imitate something before I went away, since the
night that I went into the Park, only since then."

"Somebody with a voice like that must have been here
while you were away," Father Murchison repeated, with a
gentle obstinacy.

"I'll soon find out."

Guildea pressed the bell. Pitting stole in almost
immediately.

"Pitting," said the Professor, speaking in a high, sharp
voice, "did anyone come into this room during my absence
at the sea?"

"Certainly not, sir, except the maids—and me, sir."

"Not a soul? You are certain?"

"Perfectly certain, sir."

The cold voice of the butler sounded surprised, almost
resentful. The Professor flung out his hand toward the
cage.

"Has the bird been here the whole time?"

"Yes, sir."

"He was not moved, taken elsewhere, even for a moment?"

Pitting's pale face began to look almost expressive, and his lips were pursed.

"Certainly not, sir."

"Thank you. That will do."

The butler retired, moving with a sort of ostentatious rectitude. When he had reached the door, and was just going out, his master called:

"Wait a minute, Pitting."

The butler paused. Guildea bit his lips, tugged at his beard uneasily two or three times, and then said:

"Have you noticed—er—the parrot talking lately in a— a very peculiar, very disagreeable voice?"

"Yes, sir—a soft voice like, sir."

"Ha! Since when?"

"Since you went away, sir. He's always at it."

"Exactly. Well, and what did you think of it?"

"Beg pardon, sir?"

"What do you think about his talking in this voice?"

"Oh, that it's only his play, sir."

"I see. That's all, Pitting."

The butler disappeared and closed the door noiselessly behind him.

Guildea turned his eyes on his friend.

"There, you see!" he ejaculated.

"It's certainly very odd," said the Father. "Very odd indeed. You are certain you have no maid who talks at all like that?"

"My dear Murchison! Would you keep a servant with such a voice about you for two days?"

"No."

"My housemaid has been with me for five years, my cook for seven. You've heard Pitting speak. The three of them make up my entire household. A parrot never speaks in a voice it has not heard. Where has it heard that voice?"

"But we hear nothing?"

"No. Nor do we see anything. But it does. It feels something too. Didn't you observe it presenting its head to be scratched?"

"Certainly it seemed to be doing so."

"It was doing so."

Father Murchison said nothing. He was full of increasing discomfort that almost amounted to apprehension.

"Are you convinced?" said Guildea, rather irritably.

"No. The whole matter is very strange. But till I hear, see or feel—as you do—the presence of something, I cannot believe."

"You mean that you will not?"

"Perhaps. Well, it is time I went."

Guildea did not try to detain him, but said, as he let him out:

"Do me a favor, come again tomorrow night."

The Father had an engagement. He hesitated, looked into the Professor's face and said:

"I will. At nine I'll be with you. Good-night."

When he was on the pavement he felt relieved. He turned round, saw Guildea stepping into his passage, and shivered.

V

Father Murchison walked all the way home to Bird Street that night. He required exercise after the strange and disagreeable evening he had spent, an evening upon which he looked back already as a man looks back upon a nightmare. In his ears, as he walked, sounded the gentle and intolerable voice. Even the memory of it caused him physical discomfort. He tried to put it from him, and to consider the whole matter calmly. The Professor had offered his proof that there was some strange presence in his house. Could any reasonable man accept such proof? Father Murchison told himself that no reasonable man could accept it. The parrot's proceedings were, no doubt, extraordinary. The bird had succeeded in producing an extraordinary illusion of an invisible presence in the room. But that there really was such a presence the Father insisted on denying to himself. The devoutly religious, those who believe implicitly in the miracles recorded in the Bible, and who regulate their lives by the messages they suppose themselves to receive directly from the Great Ruler of a hidden World, are seldom inclined to accept any notion of supernatural intrusion into the affairs of daily life. They put it from them with anxious determination. They regard it fixedly as hocuspocus, childish if not wicked.

Father Murchison inclined to the normal view of the devoted churchman. He was determined to incline to it. He could not—so he now told himself—accept the idea that his friend was being supernaturally punished for his lack of humanity, his deficiency in affection, by being obliged to endure the love of some horrible thing, which could not be seen, heard, or handled. Nevertheless, retribution did certainly seem to wait upon Guildea's condition. That which he had unnaturally dreaded and shrunk from in his thought he seemed to be now forced unnaturally to suffer. The Father prayed for his friend that night before the little, humble altar in the barely furnished, cell-like chamber where he slept.

On the following evening, when he called in Hyde Park Place, the door was opened by the housemaid, and Father Murchison mounted the stairs, wondering what had become of Pitting. He was met at the library door by Guildea and was painfully struck by the alteration in his appearance. His face was ashen in hue, and there were lines beneath his eyes. The eyes themselves looked excited and horribly forlorn. His hair and dress were disordered and his lips twitched continually, as if he were shaken by some acute nervous apprehension.

"What has become of Pitting?" asked the Father, grasping Guildea's hot and feverish hand.

"He has left my service."

"Left your service!" exclaimed the Father in utter amazement.

"Yes, this afternoon."

"May one ask why?"

"I'm going to tell you. It's all part and parcel of this— this most odious business. You remember once discussing the relations men ought to have with their servants?"

"Ah!" cried the Father, with a flash of inspiration. "The crisis has occurred?"

"Exactly," said the Professor, with a bitter smile. "The crisis has occurred. I called upon Pitting to be a man and a brother. He responded by declining the invitation. I upbraided him. He gave me warning. I paid him his wages and told him he could go at once. And he has gone. What are you looking at me like that for?"

"I didn't know," said Father Murchison, hastily dropping his eyes, and looking away. "Why," he added. "Napoleon is gone too."

"I sold him today to one of those shops in Shaftesbury Avenue."

"Why?"

"He sickened me with his abominable imitation of—his intercourse with—well, you know what he was at last night. I have no further need of his proof to tell me I am not dreaming. And, being convinced as I now am, that all I have thought to have happened has actually happened, I care very little about convincing others. Forgive me for saying so, Murchison, but I am now certain that my anxiety to make you believe in the presence of something here really arose from some faint doubt on that subject—within myself. All doubt has now vanished."

"Tell me why."

"I will."

Both men were standing by the fire. They continued to stand while Guildea went on:

"Last night I felt it."

"What?" cried the Father.

"I say that last night, as I was going upstairs to bed, I felt something accompanying me and nestling up against me."

"How horrible!" exclaimed the Father, involuntarily.

Guildea smiled drearily.

"I will not deny the horror of it. I cannot, since I was compelled to call on Pitting for assistance."

"But—tell me—what was it, at least what did it seem to be?"

"It seemed to be a human being. It seemed, I say; and what I mean exactly is that the effect upon me was rather that of human contact than of anything else. But I could see nothing, hear nothing. Only, three times, I felt this gentle, but determined, push against me, as if to coax me and to attract my attention. The first time it happened I was on the landing outside this room, with my foot on the first stair. I will confess to you, Murchison, that I bounded upstairs like one pursued. That is the shameful truth. Just as I was about to enter my bedroom, however, I felt the thing entering with me, and, as I have said, squeezing, with loathsome, sickening tenderness, against my side. Then—"

He paused, turned toward the fire and leaned his head on his arm. Father was greatly moved by the strange helplessness and despair of the attitude. He laid his hand affectionately on Guildea's shoulder.

"Then?"

Guildea lifted his head. He looked painfully abashed.

"Then, Murchison, I am ashamed to say, I broke down, suddenly, unaccountably, in a way I have thought wholly impossible to me. I struck out with my hands to thrust the thing away. It pressed more closely to me. The pressure, the contact became unbearable to me. I shouted out for Pitting. I—I believe I must have cried—'Help.' "

"He came, of course?"

"Yes, with his usual soft, unemotional quiet. His calm— its opposition to my excitement of disgust and horror— must, I suppose, have irritated me. I was not myself, no, no!"

He stopped abruptly. Then—

"But I need hardly tell you that," he added, with most piteous irony.

"And what did you say to Pitting?"

"I said that he should have been quicker. He begged my pardon. His cold voice really maddened me, and I burst out into some foolish, contemptible diatribe, called him a machine, taunted him, then—as I felt that loathsome thing nestling once more to me—begged him to assist me, to stay with me, not to leave me alone—I meant in the company of my tormentor. Whether he was frightened, or whether he was angry at my unjust and violent manner and speech a moment before, I don't know. In any case he answered that he was engaged as a butler, and not to sit up all night with people. I suspect he thought I had taken too much to drink. No doubt that was it. I believe I swore at him as a coward—I! This morning he said he wished to leave my service. I gave him a month's wages, a good character as a butler, and sent him off at once."

"But the night? How did you pass it?"

"I sat up all night."

"Where? In your bedroom?"

"Yes—with the door open—to let it go."

"You felt that it stayed?"

"It never left me for a moment, but it did not touch me again. When it was light I took a bath, lay down for a little while, but did not close my eyes. After breakfast I had the explanation with Pitting and paid him. Then I came up here. My nerves were in a very shattered condition. Well, I sat down, tried to write, to think. But the silence was broken in the most abominable manner."

"How?"

"By the murmur of that appalling voice, that voice of a lovesick idiot, sickly but determined. Ugh!"

He shuddered in every limb. Then he pulled himself together, assumed, with a self-conscious effort, his most determined, most aggressive, manner, and added:

"I couldn't stand that. I had come to the end of my tether; so I sprang up, ordered a cab to be called, seized the cage and drove with it to a bird shop in Shaftesbury Avenue. There I sold the parrot for a trifle. I think, Murchison, that I must have been nearly mad then, for, as I came out of the wretched shop, and stood for an instant on the pavement among the cages of rabbits, guinea pigs, and puppy dogs, I laughed aloud. I felt as if a load was lifted from my shoulders, as if in selling that voice I had sold the cursed thing that torments me. But when I got back to the house it was here. It's here now. I suppose it will always be here."

He shuffled his feet on the rug in front of the fire.

"What on earth am I to do?" he said. "I'm ashamed of myself, Murchison, but—but I suppose there are things in the world that certain men simply can't endure. Well, I can't endure this, and there's an end of the matter."

He ceased. The Father was silent. In presence of this extraordinary distress he did not know what to say. He recognized the uselessness of attempting to comfort Guildea, and he sat with his eyes turned, almost moodily, to the ground. And while he sat there he tried to give himself to the influences within the room, to feel all that was within it. He even, half-unconsciously, tried to force his imagination to play tricks with him. But he remained totally unaware of any third person with them. At length he said:

"Guildea, I cannot pretend to doubt the reality of your misery here. You must go away, and at once. When is your Paris lecture?"

"Next week. In nine days from now."

"Go to Paris tomorrow then; you say you have never had any consciousness that this—this thing pursued you beyond your own front door?"

"Never—hitherto."

"Go tomorrow morning. Stay away till after your lecture. And then let us see if the affair is at an end. Hope, my dear friend, hope."

He had stood up. Now he clasped the Professor's hand.

"See all your friends in Paris. Seek distractions. I would ask you also to seek—other help."

He said the last words with a gentle, earnest gravity and simplicity that touched Guildea, who returned his handclasp almost warmly.

"I'll go," he said. "I'll catch the ten-o clock train, and tonight I'll sleep at an hotel, at the Grosvenor—that's close to the station. It will be more convenient for the train."

As Father Murchison went home that night he kept thinking of that sentence: "It will be more convenient for the train." The weakness in Guildea that had prompted its utterance appalled him.

VI

No letter came to Father Murchison from the Professor during the next few days and this silence reassured him, for it seemed to betoken that all was well. The day of the lecture dawned and passed. On the following morning, the Father eagerly opened the *Times,* and scanned its pages to see if there were any report of the great meeting of scientific men which Guildea had addressed. He glanced up and down the columns with anxious eyes, then suddenly his hands stiffened as they held the sheets. He had come upon the following paragraph:

We regret to announce that Professor Frederic Guildea was suddenly seized with severe illness yesterday evening while addressing a scientific meeting in Paris. It was observed that he looked very pale and nervous when he rose to his feet. Nevertheless, he spoke in French fluently for about a quarter of an hour. Then he appeared to become uneasy. He faltered and glanced about like a man apprehensive, or in severe distress. He even stopped once or twice, and seemed unable to go on, to remember what he wished to say. But, pulling himself together with an obvious effort, he continued to address the audience. Suddenly, however, he paused again, edged furtively along the platform, as if pursued by something which he feared, struck out with his hands, uttered a loud, harsh cry and fainted. The sensation in the hall was indescribable. People rose from their seats. Women screamed, and, for a moment, there was a veritable panic. It is feared that the Professor's mind must have temporarily given way owing to overwork. We understand that he will return to England as soon as possible, and we sincerely hope that necessary rest and quiet will soon have the desired effect, and that he will be completely restored to health and enabled to prosecute further the investigations which have already so benefited the world.

The Father dropped the paper, hurried out into Bird Street, sent a wire of enquiry to Paris, and received the same day the following reply: "Returning tomorrow. Please call evening. Guildea." On that evening the Father called in Hyde Park Place, was at once admitted, and found Guildea sitting by the fire in the library, ghastly pale, with a heavy rug over his knees. He looked like a man emaciated by a long and severe illness, and in his wide open eyes there was an expression of fixed horror. The Father started at the sight of him, and could scarcely refrain from crying out. He was beginning to express his sympathy when Guildea stopped him with a trembling gesture.

"I know all that," Guildea said, "I know. This Paris affair—" He faltered and stopped.

"You ought never to have gone," said the Father. "I was wrong. I ought not to have advised your going. You were not fit."

"I was perfectly fit," he answered with the irritability of sickness. "But I was—I was accompanied by that abominable thing."

He glanced hastily round him, shifted his chair and pulled the rug higher over his knees. The Father wondered why he was thus wrapped up. For the fire was bright and red and the night was not very cold.

"I was accompanied to Paris," he continued, pressing his upper teeth upon his lower lip.

He paused again, obviously striving to control himself. But the effort was vain. There was no resistance in the man. He writhed in his chair and suddenly burst forth in a tone of hopeless lamentation.

"Murchison, this being, thing—whatever it is—no longer leaves me even for a moment. It will not stay here unless I am here, for it loves me, persistently, idiotically. It accompanied me to Paris, stayed with me there, pursued me to the lecture hall, pressed against me, caressed me while I was speaking. It has returned with me here. It is here now,"—he uttered a sharp cry—"now, as I sit here with you. It is nestling up to me, fawning upon me, touching my hands. Man, man, can't you feel that it is here?"

"No," the Father answered truly.

"I try to protect myself from its loathsome contact," Guildea continued, with fierce excitement, clutching the thick rug with both hands. "But nothing is of any avail against it. Nothing. What is it? What can it be? Why should it have come to me that night?"

"Perhaps as a punishment," said the Father, with a quick softness.

"For what?"

"You hated affection. You put human feeling aside with contempt. You had, you desired to have, no love for anyone. Nor did you desire to receive any love from anything. Perhaps this is a punishment."

Guildea stared into his face.

"D'you believe that?" he cried.

"I don't know," said the Father. "But it may be so. Try to endure it, even to welcome it. Possibly then the persecution will cease."

"I know it means me no harm," Guildea exclaimed, "it seeks me out of affection. It was led to me by some amazing attraction which I exercise over it ignorantly. I know that. But to a man of my nature that is the ghastly part of the matter. If it would hate me, I could bear it. If it would attack me, if it would try to do me some dreadful harm, I should become a man again. I should be braced to fight against it. But this gentleness, this abominable solicitude, this brainless worship of an idiot, persistent, sickly, horribly physical, I cannot endure. What does it want of me? What would it demand of me? It nestles to me. It leans against me. I feel its touch, like the touch of a feather, trembling about my heart, as if it sought to number my pulsations, to find out the inmost secrets of my impulses and desires. No privacy is left to me." He sprang up excitedly. "I cannot withdraw," he cried, "I cannot be alone, untouched, unworshipped, unwatched for even one-half second. Murchison, I am dying of this, I am dying."

He sank down again in his chair, staring apprehensively on all sides, with the passion of some blind man, deluded in the belief that by his furious and continued effort he will attain sight. The Father knew well that he sought to pierce the veil of the invisible, and have knowledge of the thing that loved him.

"Guildea," the Father said, with insistent earnestness,

"try to endure this—do more—try to give this thing what it seeks."

"But it seeks my love."

"Learn to give it your love and it may go, having received what it came for."

"T'sh! You talk like a priest. Suffer your persecutors. Do good to them that despitefully use you. You talk as a priest."

"As a friend I spoke naturally, indeed, right out of my heart. The idea suddenly came to me that all this—truth or seeming, it doesn't matter which—may be some strange form of lesson. I have had lessons—painful ones. I shall have many more. If you could welcome—"

"I can't! I can't!" Guildea cried fiercely. "Hatred! I can give it that—always that, nothing but that—hatred, hatred."

He raised his voice, glared into the emptiness of the room, and repeated, "Hatred!"

As he spoke, the waxen pallor of his cheeks increased until he looked like a corpse with living eyes. The Father feared that he was going to collapse and faint, but suddenly he raised himself upon his chair and said, in a high and keen voice, full of suppressed excitement:

"Murchison, Murchison!"

"Yes. What is it?"

An amazing ecstasy shone in Guildea's eyes.

"It wants to leave me," he cried. "It wants to go! Don't lose a moment! Let it out! The window—the window!"

The Father, wondering, went to the near window, drew aside the curtains and pushed it open. The branches of the trees in the garden creaked drily in the light wind. Guildea leaned forward on the arms of his chair. There was silence for a moment. Then Guildea, speaking in a rapid whisper, said:

"No, no. Open this door—open the hall door. I feel—I feel that it will return the way it came. Make haste—ah, go!"

The Father obeyed—to soothe him, hurried to the door and opened it wide. Then he glanced back to Guildea. He was standing up, bent forward. His eyes were glaring with eager expectation, and, as the Father turned, he made a furious gesture towards the passage with his thin hands.

The Father hastened out and down the stairs. As he descended in the twilight he fancied he heard a slight cry from the room behind him, but he did not pause. He flung the hall door open, standing back against the wall. After waiting a moment—to satisfy Guildea, he was about to close the door again, and had his hand on it, when he was attracted irresistibly to look forth toward the park. The night was lit by a young moon, and gazing through the railings, his eyes fell upon a bench beyond them.

Upon the bench something was sitting, huddled together very strangely.

The Father remembered instantly Guildea's description of that former night, that night of Advent, and a sensation of horror-stricken curiosity stole through him.

Was there then really something that had indeed come to the Professor? And had it finished its work, fulfilled its desire and gone back to its former existence?

The Father hesitated a moment in the doorway. Then he stepped out resolutely and crossed the road, keeping his eyes fixed upon this black or dark object that leaned so strangely upon the bench. He could not tell yet what it was like, but he fancied it was unlike anything with which his eyes were acquainted. He reached the opposite path, and was about to pass through the gate in the railings, when his arm was brusquely grasped. He started, turned round, and saw a policemen eyeing him suspiciously.

"What are you up to?" said the policeman.

The Father was suddenly aware that he had no hat upon his head, and that his appearance, as he stole forward in his cassock, with his eyes intently fixed upon the bench in the Park, was probably unusual enough to excite suspicion.

"It's all right, policeman," he answered quickly, thrusting some money into the constable's hand.

Then, breaking from him, the Father hurried toward the bench, bitterly vexed at the interruption. When he reached it, nothing was there. Guildea's experience had been almost exactly repeated and, filled with unreasonable disappointment, the Father returned to the house, entered it, shut the door and hastened up the narrow stairway into the library.

On the hearth rug, close to the fire, he found Guildea lying with his head lolled against the armchair from which he had recently risen. There was a shocking expression of terror on his convulsed face. On examining him the Father found that he was dead.

The doctor, who was called in, said that the cause of death was failure of the heart.

When Father Murchison was told this, he murmured:

"Failure of the heart! It was that, then!"

He turned to the doctor and said:

"Could it have been prevented?"

The doctor drew on his gloves and answered:

"Possibly, if it had been taken in time. Weakness of the heart requires a great deal of care. The Professor was too much absorbed in his work. He should have lived very differently."

The Father nodded.

"Yes, yes," he said, sadly.

NATURAL SELECTION

Gilbert Thomas

"HELL, I'M COOKIN' HERE," BUTTER SAID:

"Then get back in the car," Craw said.

"Damned if I will."

"Then shut up."

"Bake in the car. Fry out here."

"All right. Only shut up about it."

The fat one hesitated. "I'm sorry, Craw," he said.

"Yeah."

Craw wanted to stand up but he didn't. The sun cut

across the car at the three-o'clock angle, puddling hot
shadows next to the running board. Craw crouched there,
working on two tin containers; they were hot in his hands.
He'd been hammering and cutting at the cans for almost
an hour. He wanted to stretch his back, to look down the
road for any sign of an approaching car. But he didn't
want to face that sun.

"Take a look down the road," Craw said.

"Ain't nothing comin'," Butter said. But he put a fleshy
hand on the running board and wheezed to his feet. Craw
had that look on his face when he's mad, and Butter knew
he'd best stand up and look down the road. He did,
breathing in the scorched air, feeling it burn his face, water
his eyes. Nothing. To the north the dirt road stretched
straight and empty. To the south it wound out of sight behind the red rocks. Nothing.

"See anything?" Craw was working again.

"Not even a lizard."

"Any dust?"

"I said there was nothin'." Butter squatted full in the
slim shadow and began dabbing at his sweat with a blue
rag.

They'd started three days ago, started from a small
deserted town that had one gas station, a general store, and
no hotel. It was to be a prospecting trip, but all they really
expected to find was a good time.

Their old car had been piled high with canned food,
camping gear, tools, and bagged-water. Craw had fixed the
car before they had left. "She may be old," he'd said, "but
she'll do."

And Butter'd said, "You're the boss," because Craw had
been a mechanic in Los Angeles. But she hadn't done.
Hadn't done at all. Maybe it was because Butter had forgotten to pack the ten-quart tin of oil, and he didn't want
Craw to get mad, so he didn't tell him. Craw would sit in
the car while Butter would check the oil in the crankcase
and the water in the radiator. And Butter would always
say, "She's perkin'."

Everything might have been all right if it hadn't been for

one jagged rock that had fallen from a cliff overhanging
the road. The car had hit the rock, the rock had punctured
the crankcase. In time the motor had exploded with friction heat, two pistons punching through the cast-iron
block.

And so they waited beside their dead car, waited
through part of the canned food, all the water. Nothing
came. . . .

Craw, still crouched, still working on the tin cans, listened to the fat one's dry breathing. Butter. Everyone
called him that because of his fat. His skin, stretched
tight over his slob, was somehow yellow. Even after being
in the sun—how long had it been?—it was still somehow
yellow. Butter. Was anyone ever so fat? Butter liked greasy
soups, Butter liked fat meat, pie, potatoes, soda pop—and
slim girls. Craw wondered why he'd ever teamed up with
the ball of butter. He didn t like him. But he'd been good
for laughs, and the slim girls hadn't gone for Butter. Now,
hearing him breathing that way, and smelling his body
pouring sweat next to him in the car's shadow, and remembering the oil . . .

"Hey! You nuts?" Butter yelled, rolling out of the way of
Craw's fists.

"You stinkin' two-ton . . . !"

"Craw!"

"I'll kill you!" Craw heard his voice getting away from
him, getting higher. He felt his fists hit and disappear in
flesh. He wondered if Butter could feel it somewhere deep
under that fat, down where his bones began. It was easy.
Too easy. He stopped. And he was sorry. "You all right?"

"I'm—I'm all right," Butter said.

"Take the bottom can and drain out what's left in the
radiator."

"All right, Craw."

Butter drained the radiator and brought the rusty water
back to Craw. There wasn't much. Craw started a small
greasewood fire and began to distill the water.

"I wouldn't have thought of that, Craw," Butter said
happily.

"Someone's got to do some thinking."

"Maybe when you finish we'd better take the water and start walking back?"

"Back where?"

"Remember, maybe twenty miles back, that old house?"

"You feel like walking twenty miles?"

Butter closed his eyes and cried. But his sweat had stopped and there were no tears.

"L.A. I been thinking about L.A.," Butter said.

"L.A.," but Craw didn't say it the way the fat one had.

"You never did like it."

"It stinks."

"It's my home, Craw."

"That all you can think about."

"It's my home town."

"This is your home town now."

"No, it's not, Craw."

"Stop talking and shut up."

"I been thinking maybe I'm going to die."

"Yeah. Sure."

"Ain't you ever thought of that, Craw?"

"Everybody's got to die sometime."

"I always thought when I died it would be in L.A."

"I'm outta that town and I'm staying out," Craw said. "It never did me no good, and I'm not dying here *or* there."

"If I die, Craw, would you take me back to L.A.?"

"Yeah. Sure. If you die."

Somewhere a small animal made a sound. It was evening. Heat hung in the air, undecided, not knowing where to go, but lifting. The hard soil was the floor of an oven that would radiate heat for another three hours. Then cold.

Butter sat on the runningboard. He hawked but couldn't spit. He tongued the dust on his lips, then lifted a tin can and took a drink.

"Better start walking," Craw said. "Better start tonight."

Butter lowered the can. He shook it. Maybe a pint.

"Which way?" Butter asked.

"To the house."

"What if it's empty?"

"I thought it was your idea to walk back there?"

"I was only . . ." His voice dropped off.

"It won't be empty."

"Maybe if we went the other way?"

"To the house."

"Okay."

"Let's go," Craw said.

They left. Craw took the tin of water and walked ahead. Butter followed. They didn't look back.

All night? Had they walked all night? Or had it been a day and a night, or two days? They walked. Craw always a little in front. Butter stumbling, swinging slowly from one side of the road to the other: a soft, round pendulum. The road: hammered dirt at crazy angles and Butter stumbling. Craw could hear him breathing hard, and once the fat one whimpered, and once he cried. But they never stopped. The water was gone now—when had they had the last of it?—and they remembered nothing but the ruts hard as concrete, their ankles turning, the swing in the road ahead. But no house. Another mile, nothing ahead. Then Craw stopped.

"It's . . . up ahead." Craw didn't recognize his voice.

Butter tried to call out, but the sound he made was the whistle without the pea.

The house was the color of the dust it sat in. Lost in the desert with Butter and Craw. A monument to a man with arthritis who died there seeking a cure. Dry. Empty. They stood there and looked. The house was a shack of dry boards. Cracks between the boards. The floor had dropped at one end, throwing the room into lunacy. No furniture, but there was a frying pan on the wall near where the stove had been. On the floor was an empty bottle labeled Dr. Something's Muscle Liniment. One room, that's all it was, with a door in the front and one in the back. Craw tried to cuss and almost did as he went, half-sliding, across the slanting floor towards the back door.

Butter turned his back and sat down on the ground. He could hear Craw tearing at the back door, but he wasn't thinking of that. He was thinking of a bottle of cold beer, icy drops clinging to its sides. He was running the tip of his finger up and down the bottle, rubbing the cold drops off. He was using his fingernail to play with the sopping label, pushing it this way and that. Then the bottle in his mouth and that first rush of cold beer hitting his tongue.

There was an advertising sign in L.A. It looked like you could almost reach out and take one of the three cold, dripping glasses of beer on it. Ice cream. He liked ice cream. It was a little harder to bring that back. Yes. There was that place on Beverly Blvd. almost next to Western. They had ice cream and he'd always pay extra for the second scoop. Vanilla, that was good to think about: strawberry, chocolate, please, anybody, L.A.!

"Look at this," Craw tried to say.

Butter didn't look up.

"Look," and Craw dropped the can next to Butter.

Butter turned and reached for it.

"Kerosene," Craw said. "Lousy kerosene in that can. Only thing in the place. Found it underneath the car."

"Car?"

"In back."

Butter started to his feet. Craw pushed him back.

"No use looking."

"I want to see."

Craw kicked at the kerosene can, then he reached down and hoisted Butter to his feet.

Yes, there was the car. It was standing on a small rise back of the house. There were ruts leading up to it. Whoever had left it there had used the same spot to park it all the time. The car was old.

They tried to push it. It wouldn't move. The sun, the air: they had dried up every pat of grease in the car. And there was no gas.

A solid chunk of sun-dried metal, derelict, standing on a small rise in the sun. The tires were solid rubber, the kind a smart man uses on the back roads of the desert. The spokes of the wheels had been yellow, but now they were gray, bare wood with tracings of yellow near the hubs. The car was high and narrow, the kind you seldom see in this country any more, the kind you see in Mexico. It had four doors.

Craw opened one of the doors. It opened with difficulty —it needed grease. He sat behind the thick wooden steering wheel. He pulled at the gears. Everything seemed in perfect order, but dry, not rusted.

He climbed out of the car and pushed past Butter, who stood grotesquely in a squashy slump. He didn't know why, but he wanted a look at that motor. Open the hood—that's right, it comes hard, but it's open. Looks okay. Wiring?—okay. Four cylinders. Sparks? Couldn't tell yet. But even two would do. Maybe more sparks under seat, or in the tool kit. Tools? Yes, there are tools. Simple tools. But then it's a simple car. Check oil?—dry. Battery? Dead, sure. Generator brushes: sure, that's why it was always parked on this rise. If that battery ever went dead, a good push would send it rolling down; then throw her into gear and kick the clutch and she'd start. Wonder would she run on the juice generated by the brushes in the generator? And a car could run on kerosene. He'd seen it. Plenty of noise and smoke, but it could run. And they had kerosene—at least three gallons, maybe five. Enough to get somewhere. And Craw knew they'd better get somewhere, soon.

The two men sat on the broken steps that led down from the back door of the shack. It was evening again.

"Maybe, if we went back, and . . ." Butter tried to talk.

Craw knew what he meant. "Get parts out of our car?"

"That's what I meant."

Craw tried to lift his arm. It was heavy. "You want to try?" he said, but his mind was probing the old car, and Butter.

Butter's intelligence ran to fat, and by the time that was fed there wasn't much left for the brain. Should have checked the oil myself; he always makes mistakes, so it was my fault, if it was anybody's. Too tired to beat him up any more.

And now Craw knew he was going to die, and no one was going to know about it, and that wasn't the way he'd planned on dying at all. Only Butter would know, and he was going to die too. . . .

Butter had stopped thinking of cool things. As he sat there, dying: "I wish . . . I was . . . in L.A."

The old car stood high and bright in the moonlight. It was ten-thirty-eight when Craw asked: "How much you weigh?"

"Three hunnert . . . twenty," Butter said, after a while.

It was past midnight.

"Help me," Craw said, rising.

The fat one sat with his arms around his knees, rolling to and fro on his roundness. He looked like he might be moaning softly to himself, but he wasn't.

". . . with the car," Craw said. He pulled Butter to his feet with surprising strength.

He opened the hood again and began to feel the motor with his fingers, probing with his fingertips the places he had been probing with his mind. Feeling where the power would be.

"Rocks," he said. "Get rocks to put under the axle."

Trancelike the fat one wandered off to do as he was told.

All that night there was no sound but the sound of the fat one's breathing, and the clink and hammer and tap of metal on metal, as Craw worked. He knew this would be their last night. And he worked. . . .

The car was up on the rocks, its wheels pulled off. The motor lay open. Wires, plugs, and metal tubes lay patterned evenly, professionally, on the hard earth. There were small mounds of nuts and bolts heaped carefully on the running boards. The sky was purple with morning.

Butter spasmed in his sleep. Craw stood looking at him, asleep there, then he turned and started for the shack. He walked surprisingly fast. Next to the rear door there was a heavy, round, oversize oil drum that came up as high as his chest. It had a small hole in the bottom for a draft. It had been used as an incinerator.

"Whose house he in?" the old man asked.

"Up Ned's place," a woman answered.

"Funniest-lookin' car I ever saw," someone said.

"Think I saw it 'round here some years back," someone said.

"Out of his head?"

"Plumb crazy, Les said."

"Wonder how he ever got that tub out of the desert?"

It was a small town, a desert town, with one gas station, a general store, and no hotel. Now there was a cluster of people gathered around an old car parked next to the gas station. Nothing ever happened in this town, and now something was happening; so they asked questions.

"Doc's over lookin' after him," the woman said. She wore a hat and seemed to know more about it than anybody else.

"Whee!" that from a small boy, maybe ten. "It stinks."

"Yeah, don't it now," the old man said, examining the car.

"Doc think he'll live?"

"Said it all depended on how long he'd been in the desert," the woman said. "He might die."

The sun was up and it was coming down hot. The old car wasn't in the shade. The small boy made a face and held his nose, then ran to the general store for a bottle of pop. The woman with the hat left, then the rest began moving away.

Craw made his way toward the gas station, toward the car. The doctor had wanted him to rest longer, but he couldn't rest. Now he knew what he had to do.

"You all right, Buddy?" That from the man at the gas station.

"Is the car here?"

"We got lots of cars," he said. "Which one you mean?"

"The . . . old one. The . . ."

But the man interrupted. "Hey, ain't you the guy that came drivin' the old buggy off the desert? Sure, I wouldn't have recognized you," he said. "You *want* that car?"

"Where is it?"

"If you want to sell it for junk . . ."

"Where's the car?"

Then Craw saw it, standing by the road. He had the gas station attendant put gas in it.

"You're going to drive this wreck out of here?"

"Finished with that gas?"

"Yeah, but I'd better check the oil . . ."

"I've got all I need."

"Water's okay. Say, what'd you have down in that radiator . . ."

"Here's your money."

"Where you heading, Buddy?"

"L.A.," Craw said.

"Hey, you nuts?" the gas station man said. "You'll never make it."

"I'll make it," Craw said.

SIMONE
Joan Vatsek

TED FIELDING LOOKED WITH DISTASTE AT HIS SANDALED feet as they sank into the hot Egyptian sand of Alexandria's long white beach, known as *la plage* to all of Alexandria. The sandals were woven of bright leather thongs, flamboyant, expensive, and not in the least to his liking. Simone had given them to him, insisting that he wear them.

"You must, *mon chéri*. There is broken glass in the sand, always. You must not take chances. Wear them because I wish it." He resented this, feeling somehow that a man's feet should be his own; nevertheless he wore them.

They walked indolently across the hot sand, Ted and Simone and her husband, Georges, Simone setting the pace. Ted's gaze strayed to her carefully pedicured feet in the wedge cork sandals, and beyond them to those of her husband. She didn't worry about Georges stepping on glass, apparently. He was barefoot. Before them pranced the great Danes, straining at the leash that Simone held, making dancing dabs and hollows in the sand.

"My ladies-in-waiting," she called the dogs, introducing them gravely as "the only female friends I can trust. Lift your paw, Zara! *N'est-elle pas comme il faut?* Now, Shireen!"

At this command, the sad brutes would lift one heavy paw and place it in the unwilling palm of the new acquaintance, gazing up with melancholy eyes. Simone was fond of sitting in a chair with one dog on either side of her on the floor, her thin, delicate hands playing in the scruff of each neck while the animals closed their eyes or turned their heads majestically toward her. Simone and her dogs invariably caused a stir at *la plage,* the same momentary ripple among the idlers on the beach that was caused by a novel coiffure, a chic bathing suit, a new man, or a new inflated rubber toy. This exclusive section of the beach was owned by people who would meet again in Paris or on the Riviera, when it was no longer fashionable to be in Egypt. There they would greet each other with artificial surprise and pleasure, and settle down to the same social round as before.

La plage, Ted had discovered, meant a day-long orgy of dalliance and gossip; it meant reclining on mats beneath enormous, protecting umbrellas. There were games of darts and parchesi and, for some, endless bridge games on the porches of beach cabins. For others there was mild but steady gambling. There were drinks always and lavish food served at regular intervals by the Arab Soffragi. Sunbathing was a ritual at *la plage,* and the visitors swam lazily in the warm Mediterranean waves that broke on the Egyptian shore with only a whisper of sound and little foam.

It struck Ted unpleasantly that the beach was crowded with people in various stages of playful assault and entwinement, like a mass of stirring crawfish or lobsters in the hot sun.

And picking her way delicately among them was Simone, indifferent to the comments. Her head on her long neck was slightly smaller than one expected, her one fault.

Her eyes were dark, her lips mobile, her almond skin smooth, soft, luminous. She had only to walk across the sand like this to make men aware of her. They would turn to watch and their eyes would cling to the motions of her hips and to her long, tireless legs.

The edge of the short white beach coat she wore flicked against him. In one corner of it was a red-and-gold monogram. The same emblem decorated the entrance hall of her apartment, which was like a museum, with a suit of armor and a lance in one corner, massive furniture heavy with lions' paws, and a great shield over the fireplace with the escutcheon in beaten silver.

What a ridiculous room, he had thought, the first time Georges had invited him to dinner there.

That had been two months before, when he had been hired to decorate Georges's jewelry store on the rue Zaghloul, the main shopping street of Alexandria. Georges wanted a modern exterior and, inside, a glass counter suspended from the ceiling.

"Like this," Georges had said, pointing to a picture in an American magazine. "That is why I send for a bright young man. From a good American architect's firm. I take only the best."

Georges could afford the best. The jewelry store was his, as the apartment was Simone's. He was of a Swiss family of watchmakers and jewelers. Ted wondered how he ever had tangled with Simone.

She must have married him for his money, of course. Georges had married her and had wound up doing exactly what she wanted, just as Ted was doing now, staying on in Alexandria to be near her.

Yet there was more to the marriage between the respectable Georges and the vivid Simone than the money that was involved. Other wealthy men must have wanted to marry her; why, then, had she settled for Georges? There was a powerful tie between them; it was obvious when they were together.

Simone turned her head slightly, as if sensing his thoughts.

She let her eyes pass casually up his strong, tanned body to his red hair, then come to rest on his mouth before she looked into his eyes and smiled at him.

She shrugged and let her glance shift to the open bay and the blue sky. There was an island in the middle of the bay, and a few sailing skiffs tacked diligently back and forth to the shore.

His glance followed hers, and he felt a sudden longing for the open sea. It would be good to be on a ship now, headed for home.

If only he could get away from Simone! But even when he wasn't with her, he was thinking about her. While he thought about her, he never could leave Alexandria.

With each step, he was conscious of the sandals. He wanted to kick them off, plunge into the water, and swim out as far as the island.

"Think I'll swim to the island," he said.

"Mais, chéri, what is there when you get to the island?"

"I'm going for the swim," he said shortly.

"I'll go with you," Georges said. In the water, Georges was a different man, a powerful, easy swimmer who would roll and float in the water for hours.

Simone turned to Georges and frowned.

"La, mush aus die," she said in Arabic, a habit of hers which amused a great many people. "You stay with me, Georges. I won't be deserted by both of you."

She paused, waiting for Ted to leave, while Georges stood silently beside her. Ted looked at them and felt a sharp stab of jealousy. Simone raised her eybrows.

"Eh bien, chéri," she said. "Why don't you go?"

He turned and started toward the water.

The last thing he saw, from the corner of his eye, was the pull of the great Danes and the flutter of her beach coat as she started off again.

Simone made a point of being Rumanian. She had even invented a relationship between her ancestors and the ancestors of an ancient Roman family. The Rumanian language was, of course, like French or Spanish, a descendant of Latin. But the rest of her family story, like the crest she had placed on everything, was a product of her lively imagination.

The paneled dining room, in which dinner had been served to all of them that first evening Ted met them, had that same false feudal atmosphere. And so did Georges's study.

When Simone had said good-night to Ted that night, she had pressed his hand in a way that was recognizably different from courtesy. In the dim hall light her face seemed to shine as she said. "Well, then, I will pick you up tomorrow at the hotel and we shall explore Alexandria. For my husband it has ceased to be of interest. But we sightseers, you and I—" She smiled and withdrew her hand. They had been talking all evening of Europe, and of skiing in Switzerland.

After that, she had planned everything so that they could be alone together—or nearly alone. Until two weeks before, when Ted's job was done and he should have been leaving for America, Georges had gone to Cairo for two days on business.

Simone had asked Ted to supper that night, to keep her company in the great rococo room, and they had drunk tiny glasses of iced cordials until, hearing a noise and thinking that Georges had returned home unexpectedly, he had started up in sudden panic. Simone gave a lazy order in Rumanian and the two great dogs moved toward him.

They pulled him down before he reached the door, throwing him to the softly carpeted floor and standing over him until Simone spoke again, and reluctantly they had permitted him to rise.

Laughing then, she suggested that they go to her rooms to bandage a scratch on his hand. Stiffly, concealing his fury, he had refused.

"I must go!" he said, and Simone smiled and shrugged her shoulders.

"As you like, *chéri*."

It was only after the heavy front door closed behind him that he realized what she had meant. For a moment he had stood regretting his own stupidity. But it was too late to go back.

The next day he telephoned and was informed that Georges was returning that afternoon.

"But I have plans, *chéri,* amusing plans," Simone said. "And Georges has agreed. Now that you are finished with the store, we want you to build us a villa in the desert, with tennis courts, a swimming pool, screened porches. You must come to dinner and we shall talk about it."

For two weeks now he had been making sketches for Simone's villa, working in her home while Simone stretched out lazily on a couch, criticizing, approving. They had not been completely alone again since that night.

But while Georges was always present, he seemed perfectly amiable to have Ted stay as long as he pleased. He said that he was willing to sign the contract for the villa whenever Ted wished.

The villa would keep Ted in Alexandria for at least a year longer.

If he signed the contract, he would have to resign his job at home. And after the year was finished, what would happen? Yet it would be a year with Simone, a year in which Georges could not always be present.

Viciously Ted kicked off his sandals and waded into the warm water. He was tingling pleasantly by the time he reached the island. He stood near the shore, breathing hard, feeling refreshed and whole.

And the first thing he did was to look for Simone's cabin, shading his eyes with his hand.

There it was, with its white and blue awnings; there lay Zara and Shireen on either side of the steps. He could see Abduh the Soffragi moving about on the porch, setting the table. He could not see either Simone or Georges. The thought that perhaps they were in the little cabin together made him shift uneasily and finally dive back into the water and swim furiously to the cabin.

Georges was seated in a beach chair on the porch. From the neck down he looked like a modest Buddha. A habitual blankness and concealment in his face canceled any expression of his thoughts.

"You have had a good swim, my young friend?" he asked.

"Yes, thanks."

Georges returned to his paper.

Abduh had set out dishes of *apéritifs* and was opening a bottle of beer with a dexterous flick of his black hand.

Ted nodded to him and stepped into the cabin to change.

Simone was there. She was sitting at her dressing table, and he caught sight of her face in the mirror before she swiftly turned, rose, and clasped her arms about his neck, pressing against his wet body. Her hair hung loose and dark at her neck and she smelled of some delicate powder.

"Simone!" he whispered, glancing toward the door.

She released him swiftly but remained close to him, tantalizing him. They could hear the clinking of beer bottles and the rustle of Georges's newspaper.

He seized her and drew her close again, holding her tighter and tighter in a fierce, demanding embrace.

She struggled, pushing at him with her hands and laughing softly. Since Georges came back she had been playing with him this way. *Chéri . . . mais, chéri!* Later . . . later." She broke away with a quick twist of her body. "Be patient," she whispered again. "Later."

Later, he thought. What did she mean by later? Had she some plan? Was Georges going away again? Since his return Georges had been watching them like a hawk, or rather more like an owl, round-eyed, knowing, determined to keep them in his sight.

Simone lifted the curtain that hung at the door and said in a tone that was merely careless and discontented, "I can do nothing with my hair."

"It is well enough," said Georges. "Would you like some of the paper?"

"Merci, non. All that violence."

"I find it soothing," said Georges. "For you it is too far away, *non?"*

She laughed. "What things you say," she said.

Ted suddenly knew something about them that he had been aware of even on that first evening, when she had lazily flirted with him and every once in a while had let her eyes slide toward Georges, as if seeking his reaction. Sometimes he felt like a football between them, necessary to their game.

He forgot all of this when he held her in his arms, when they were alone together, even when he was in the same room with her, hearing the sound of her voice as now. At times like this nothing else seemed to matter.

He had talked of her getting a divorce, coming with him to America, but she had merely tapped him playfully and murmured, "Dear Teddie—"

As though she would give up Georges and the jewelry shop on the rue Zaghlol for him! In the meantime he was risking a good job, jeopardizing his whole career, for her sake.

As if he were already out of work and wondering what to do next, he stormed out onto the porch. Simone was nibbling on a pickle, and Georges's mouth was ringed with beer foam. They both stared at him in surprise.

"What is the matter, *chéri?*" Simone asked.

"Nothing," he said. "Nothing at all."

"How unsettled you are!" she exclaimed. "Have something to eat. Here."

She offered him a black olive. Inwardly resisting, he took it with his mouth. She let her fingers linger, and involuntarily, without intending to, he gave them a little bite. Simone's glance slipped to her husband. Georges was watching them. Ted, turning his head, caught the expression of suppressed torment on his face.

Simone kept offering him tidbits after that and she seemed excited and pleased when he accepted them. She talked rapidly and kept filling their glasses with an even measure of beer.

Zara and Shireen lay in giant lethargy beneath the striped awning in front of the cabin, streaks of light on their hides. They came to life when Simone threw them chunks of meat that they tore crunched and growled over until nothing was left but the bones, which Abduh gathered up after clearing the table.

With the advent of noon, the beach had cleared, as if by

magic, only mats, umbrellas, oversized balls, and other expensive playthings left on the sands. A general siesta invariably followed the elaborate luncheons.

Georges was nodding sleepily and Simone prepared his bunk for him.

He went in yawning, after an almost imperceptible glance at Ted, who sat staring moodily out to sea.

Simone returned and perched beside him on the cushioned bench. Her hand ran gently along his arm. She said nothing. He did not look at her. The tightening of a long muscle in his arm, like the string of a violin, was his involuntary response to her touch.

"Simone, I must go," he said.

"Ah? Then you must, *chéri.*"

He turned to look at her so abruptly that she nearly lost her balance. He caught her, and she smiled at him. His arms tightened and he put his head against her and closed his eyes.

She began to ruffle his hair gently. The caressing fingers recalled to him the way she would play in the scruff of Zara's neck.

He lifted his head angrily.

"How alike we are!" she exclaimed. "One moment you are happy, you trust me, you are content; the next you are furious, bitter!" She slipped her arm around his neck and let her hand hang loosely on his breast. It was like the exquisite trophy, he thought, of some African chief wearing the teeth of a lion or the claws of a tigress.

"You give me the strangest fancies," he said.

"You give me fancies, too, *chéri,*" she replied, "only there is nothing strange about them."

Would he ever be able to forget the sound of her voice, that deep-throated purr?

He lifted her hand to his lips and kissed the palm, the delicate wrist, the inner softness of her arm, knowing all the while that he should leave her. He could go this very afternoon. There was an American freighter that took on a few passengers, sailing that afternoon. The thought of it had been in the back of his mind ever since Georges mentioned it. One of his clerks had been scheduled to leave on it, but his passport had not come through, yet Ted's passport was in order; he might leave at any time.

"Simone," he said, "what are we going to do?"

She looked startled, "We?" Her voice echoed his. "Ah, what can we do?"

"Come with me!"

"You are so young," she said. "Only twenty-six!"

"What has that to do with it?"

"Everything."

She turned her head away, but he could see that she was shaking a little with laughter. Furiously he spun her about.

"Hush," she said before he could speak. "Let me see if Georges is asleep."

She left him, and he could hear her moving about inside. He threw away one cigarette and lit another before she returned.

She knelt down beside him. "Darling," she murmured. "Darling, darling, darling. Georges is asleep."

She stood up and stretched. "Ah!" she yawned, as though half overcome with fatigue and half inclined to stay with him.

He made as if to catch hold of her, but she evaded him and with a glance over her shoulder stepped into the cabin. He hesitated. He did not want to be in there with her, with Georges so close to them.

He lifted the curtain.

"Come out, Simone," he whispered. "Where are you?"

"Here, *chéri*." The odor of perfume came to him as he stepped in, reaching for her, and found her suddenly in his arms, pressing against him.

She drew down his head on her mouth, and for an instant he lost all track of time and place. Then he came to his senses, straightened, and tried to pull her arms away from his neck, but she would not let him.

"He's asleep," she whispered. "Asleep—asleep."

It came to him with an electric shock that Simone was in some perverse way enjoying Georges's closeness to them.

His rising intensity ebbed away and he tried to push her from him.

She clung to him tenaciously. He could see her blind face with the closed eyes and parted lips.

"Simone!" He shook her.

She kept on murmuring, as if it were a delightful song, "He's asleep, asleep, asleep."

"How can you be so sure?" he asked, stepping back to search her face. There was a crash behind him. He had backed into her dressing table and knocked off one of the perfume bottles. It broke and sent an overpowering odor into the room. The noise seemed deafening.

He glanced at the curtain of Georges's bed. It did not stir. There was no movement behind it, no sound.

"You see?" Simone said, with triumph in her voice. "He is quite harmless, *chéri*."

"You gave him something! You put something in his brandy!"

She shrugged. "And what if I did?" she asked softly. "Was it not clever of me?"

Her arms twined around his neck again.

"You devil!" he shouted. Suddenly he had had enough, enough of the dark little cabin with the sleeping man, the sickening perfume, Simone sidling up to him. He knew that he was through with her. If she could do this to him today she could do anything to any man.

He wrenched her arms away and made for the door.

"*Chéri!*" she cried.

He rushed down the steps and past the sleeping dogs.

"Teddie!" she cried from the top of the steps. She had seized a robe and stood there, looking wild-eyed and disheveled.

He ran lightly along the beach. He felt unaccountably lighthearted. It had been so much easier than he had expected. He would not even have to say good-by to her now. He would just keep on walking and never come back.

Let her think that he was merely taking a walk on the beach, and that he would return to her later.

He came to the queer formation of rocks that was called the Devil's Hole, great boulders flung upon the beach forming a crater in the center, through which the sea came rushing at full tide.

He clambered over the pile of rock and paused beside the crater to glance at the cabin.

Simone was running, stumbling down the beach with her robe caught around her, and Zara and Shireen loped along at her side. So she knew this was different. She had remembered the ship leaving that afternoon. He could just make it—if she let him. If the dogs let him, he thought grimly. There was no mistake of her intention. She meant to have the dogs pull him down, as she had once before. She was urging them on, exciting them. He could hear her shrill commands, see the dogs break into a gallop.

He scrambled hastily down the other side of the rocks. He felt a distant fear. If she won now, if the dogs pulled him down on the languorous beach once more, he might let the next ship sail without him after all. He had to escape today.

He sped across the stretch of clean sand. There were no cabins here; the waves came up higher, leaving shorn bits of seaweed and sharp edges of clams, wrecks of starfish.

The dogs clambered to the top of the rocks. He glanced back in time to see them hurl themselves into the air, leaping from the cliffs to the sand and starting after him with giant lopes. They were gaining on him, coming nearer and nearer, their excited baying close upon him. Even Simone could not stop them now.

But he knew she would not try to stop them. She would let them overtake him and maul him, perhaps kill him, rather than give him another chance to escape from her.

He had only one chance. He could not reach the next stairway up to the street level. He must attempt to scale the sheer wall rising sharply from the beach to the banked asphalt avenue above.

Desperately he swerved and made for the wall.

He jumped with his foot against it and hurled himself upward, barely catching the top of it with one hand, then the other, clinging by his fingers. The dogs rushed up, leaping high, after him, their claws scratching the wall. If he dropped now, he was done for. There was savagery in their maddened yelping.

If he did fall, and they killed him before help arrived, it would be a regrettable accident. He could see it in the papers, *a regrettable accident*. No real inquiry would be made into the case. Georges's local influence would see to that. It seemed, suddenly, an utterly abject and useless way to die.

Weak from his violent effort, he clung there, capable only of holding on. He couldn't lift himself over. He could feel his shoulders twisting with his own weight as his fingers clutched the cement. He could feel the hot breath of the dogs on his feet.

The snapping of the dog's teeth scraped his ankle. It galvanized him suddenly, gave him the strength he needed.

He braced the wall with one swinging foot, gave a push, and threw himself up, pulling up the rest of the way until his bare feet hit the firm, fiery pavement. He lay there exhausted and panting.

He could hear the wild yelping of the dogs sink into a whimper, and he turned to look down at them as they leaped high and struck their bodies against the wall.

Simome came running up, her face flushed and distorted.

She called out something to him, but her words were drowned by the clamor of the dogs, and in her furiously flushed face he saw no trace of the beauty he once had found there.

He turned his back on her, stepped away from the wall, hailed a taxi, and jumped in. He leaned back, still dripping with perspiration. He found that he was grinning unnaturally to himself. He felt wonderfully free and alive.

It took only ten minutes to change, fling his things into a bag, and check out of the hotel. Within an hour he was pacing up and down the deck of the American freighter, picking his way through the marine clutter that smelled comfortably of tar, past two sailors tacking down the tarpaulin over the hold.

He paced up and down with the uneasiness of a pris-

oner, not yet sure of his freedom. The gangplank still
stretched across the narrow span of water separating the
ship from the dock. If Simone found he had left his hotel,
he was sure she would have no scruples about following
him here. What could he do then?

When the gangplank was hauled in and he saw the span
widening as the ship slowly pulled away, he felt a mingling
of bitter regret and relief. Now it was certain that he never
would see her again.

But when they were still near enough to make out the
shapes of the figures ashore, the unmistakable trio, Simone
and the great Danes, dashed out upon the dock.

The dogs ran snuffling and whimpering to the farthest tip
of the dock, then back again to the still figure in the white
robe with the emblem, that slowly dwindled as the ship
moved away.

She did not move or lift her hand, nor did he. She only
stood there as long as she could see the ship, and he the
shore.

He went below with a slowly gathering feeling of thank-
fulness. There was no longer any regret. In his cabin he un-
packed, then lay on his bunk and smoked luxuriously.

The greater the distance the churning engines of the
freighter put between them, the more clearly could he see
the enormity of Simone's intent. Why, she was capable of
anything! She would not only have let those damned dogs
kill him, she would positively have relished it!

Slowly he relaxed. The vibration of the ship lulled him
into a grateful doze, but he woke from it abruptly, for the
sudden silence was overwhelming—both engines had
stopped.

He sat up groggily, glanced out the porthole. A smart-
looking empty launch was tethered alongside the freighter,
lazily riding the waves. Some last-minute visit by a customs
official.

He was still standing yawning by the porthole, savoring
his freedom, and glad that he was aboard a freighter,
where there would be no dressing for dinner or other for-
malities, when there was a knock on the cabin door.

"Come in!" he called. He hadn't heard himself speak without strain like that, for months.

"The police, Monsieur!" a frightened voice called. Ted frowned and swung open the door. What the devil! His passport was in order.

The little Greek steward stood cringingly beside two Egyptian policemen and a plainclothesman who politely presented his open wallet and then flicked it shut.

"There's nothing wrong with my passport," Ted said, exasperated. "Here, I'll get it."

"This is not a matter of *un passeport*, Monsieur," the detective said. His face was of a yellowish jaundiced cast under his tarbush, and his brown eyes were keen. "We must detain you, Monsieur, on a charge of murder."

"Murder! Who has been murdered?" Ted felt, and acted, stupefied.

"Monsieur!" the voice was reproachful, almost playful. "Monsieur Delescu, of course. Madame Delescu states that you boast you have put sleeping tablets in Monsieur Delescu's beer. Then, in the same cabin where he was sleeping, Monsieur, you attempt to attack Madame. Fortunately, she have two powerful dogs. There were many witnesses who saw them pursuing you, Monsieur."

"But—she was trying to—" he broke off. Who would believe him? "But it isn't true!" he cried, the blood hot in his face. "It was Simone who put the sleeping pills in his beer!"

"Madame Georges is in the *hôpital*, receiving treatment for shock," the man said with a touch of reverence and pity that gave a clue to what would happen in the courtroom.

"Please to pack and come!" he rapped out.

Dazedly Ted gathered up his belongings.

What chance would he have against Simone, with beauty, wealth, influence, and rage to hurl against him? And what an exquisite pleasure it would be for her, to destroy him!

BESTSELLERS
FROM DELL

fiction